THE RAKISH DUKE AND HIS SPINSTER

The Rules of Scandal 3

TESSA BROOKMAN

Chapter One

We heard that the Masked Rogue of London is fond of women with red hair. How scandalous! — excerpt from The Londoner.

Lady Natalie Reeves raised her eyes to the graying skies, and her eyebrows furrowed ever so slightly. "The weather is especially changeful this week. Do you not think so, Hannah?"

When she did not get a response, she turned to find her cousin hurrying toward a puppet player's stall, her dark curls bouncing behind her. Shaking her head whilst marveling at Hannah's excitability, she began to walk along the Serpentine. She could follow Hannah and watch the puppets amongst the growing crowd but she would much rather walk in solitude, for there was a lot that occupied her thoughts.

At nine-and-twenty, she was unmarried and had no prospects, life in London was growing more difficult by the day, and society events had become a tedious and costly affair. She had come to Hyde Park at an unfashionable hour for some fresh air—not that London was ever in an abundance of it—but the sight of blushing young ladies in the company of charming gentlemen tightened her throat.

Natalie turned her eyes away from the discomposing sight, but then she thought she heard someone call her name. Her steps slowed, and she listened, unsure.

"Lady Natalie," the voice said again, prompting her to turn around to see Miss Alexandra Gilmore, a pretty and famous daughter of Viscount Wenthorne, walking toward her. "How splendid to see you here. I almost did not recognize you, for we are hardly afforded the privilege of seeing you out of doors lately." Her blue gaze traveled over Natalie, and the corners of her mouth tilted upward in condescension.

Alexandra was the sort of lady that poets wrote about. She represented prime English beauty with golden ringlets framing a well-proportioned face, bright blue eyes, and pale flawless skin that had never seen a freckle. Her appearance was quite the opposite of Natalie's. She acknowledged Alexandra with a nod.

"Seeing you walking all alone," Alexandra continued, "one would think England had no men left. Perhaps you would like to join us." She pointed behind her at a tall gentleman who had his back to them and was speaking to another man. Natalie knew Alexandra only made that offer to show her that she commanded the attention of a gentleman of consequence. He turned very slightly but his face was shielded by his hat.

He was powerfully built, however, and his imposing height quite distinguished him. "No, I am happy walking by myself," Natalie murmured, her unease growing. She had never been able to properly defend herself whenever her spinsterhood was confronted.

Alexandra never missed the opportunity to remind her that she was a spinster, and that she would likely remain so for the rest of her life. As harsh as the words were, they were true.

"As a matter of fact, I am with my cousin," Natalie added in a late defensive attempt.

"Lord Clifford?" Alexandra asked, raising one elegant eyebrow.

"No, Miss Hannah Reeves," she replied, pointing to her cousin at the puppet player's stall.

"Oh, I was hoping it would be Lord Clifford. He, too, is rarely seen outside. Is he well?" Alexandra inclined her head as she continued her abasing examination of Natalie.

She clenched her teeth as she replied, "Yes, he is very well."

"Well, Lady Natalie, I think you ought to spend time with other people. Miss Reeves will be married soon, and..." Alexandra allowed her voice to trail off as a grin spread across her face, certain that Natalie had captured her meaning.

Hannah will marry, and you will be left alone. She swallowed miserably. It was only a matter of time before she lost even more confidence. And once her cousin, George—who became the Earl of Clifford after her father's passing—married, she would have no one. Lord help her if the new Lady Clifford wouldn't be generous enough to allow her to continue to stay with them.

Unable to continue standing there and listening to Alexandra's insults, Natalie turned to continue walking, but Alexandra placed a hand on her shoulder, stopping her. It would be inappropriate to brush the hand off and walk away, for the park was beginning to fill as the fashionable hour approached, and manners must be minded no matter what.

"Allow me to offer you some advice, Lady Natalie." Alexandra leaned close to her. "Seek a little adventure while you can. I am sure there is a gentleman out there who would want you. Who knows..." she allowed a delicate shrug, "The Masked Rogue might find you...fascinating."

Natalie's eyes widened at that insult. The Masked Rogue of London was a man with a dark reputation. Society had tried for six years to unmask him to no avail. He lived in hopeless depravity, gambling and making merry nearly every night, and word was that he had ruined many a young lady over the years. News was published daily about him, and the paper that carried the most about him was The Londoner.

So, this is my worth in society's eyes. Something to be toyed with by the Masked Rogue. Gravely wounded, she decided to leave immediately. Pulling her shoulder away so Alexandra's hand fell, she began to turn, but then her eyes caught something that froze both her blood and faculties, whilst making her heart pound fiercely against her small ribs.

The gentleman accompanying Alexandra had just turned, and Natalie recognized him as Jasper Fitzhugh, the Duke of Amsthorne, and the man who ruined her reputation nine years ago. Knowledge of what had happened was not made public, thankfully, but it had made way for the events that led to her spinsterhood to occur.

His presence halted Alexandra's condemnation but Natalie wanted the ground to open so she could hide. "Ladies," he murmured with a slight tilt of his head. Alexandra placed her hand possessively in the crook of his elbow and smiled at Natalie before turning her fluttering lashes up at him.

An enraged shiver ran down her back, because Jasper looked at her as though he had never seen her before. In fact, he smiled cordially at her, then looked down at Alexandra, waiting for her to introduce him. When she did not, he proceeded to introduce himself, which was not done.

"I am the Duke of Amsthorne," he said with a small smile. He was even more handsome than she remembered, and although she had seen him in ballrooms and gardens, she had not been this close to him since the night he stole her future and doomed her.

Grinding her teeth, she curtsied politely, offering him her hand and murmuring, "Lady Natalie Reeves." She watched his eyes, hoping to see recognition flare in their blue depths but nothing happened. Either he was pretending to have no recollection of that night, or he truly did not remember her.

Natalie was unsure which pained her more. Young and naive, she had acted upon the feelings that had grown in her heart. She allowed Jasper to lead her away from the ballroom to a private place where he charmed and tried to kiss her. Her body was filled with flutters, and she closed her eyes, ready to be kissed and begin a new life with him. Then his friend Oliver Bargrave appeared from behind a sofa, laughing as he revealed that it was all a joke.

Oliver had dared Jasper to lure an innocent girl out of the ballroom, and he accepted and carried out the plan. For them, it was all a moment of amusement, but Natalie's nightmares had begun that night. That simple jest brought on incidents that consumed her family's fortune and threw them into heavy debt.

Now, Jasper bowed over her hand, strangely oblivious to her misfortune. "It is a pleasure to make your acquaintance, My Lady." Alexandra glared at her, but Natalie found no satisfaction at the moment. She struggled to understand how he could not remember her. "And allow me to apologize for Miss Gilmore's behavior."

Natalie frowned. He had heard? It was possible because he had been standing within earshot. He looked down at Alexandra, his expression impassive.

"My aunt and I often talk about how it costs nothing to be polite. One might find it advantageous to show more respect to those who rank higher in society. Do you not think so, *Miss* Gilmore?" Alexandra's hold of his arm slackened as her face colored, seemingly in anger and humiliation.

His expression remained inscrutable, and Natalie was tempted to appreciate him defending her. She also felt the urge to tell him that she did not require his help before storming off.

Jasper regarded her for a moment before he tilted his head again, starting over, "As I was saying, it was a pleasure making your acquaintance, Lady Natalie." He began to steer Alexandra away. "Please excuse us."

Instead of Natalie walking away after having the final word, she watched them leave, her gut turning with a hundred different emotions, of which she could only identify two. Anger and shame. It was in this state that Hannah found her.

"Natalie, are you well?" she asked as she came to stand in front of her, holding a ballerina puppet. "You look pale." Her green eyes were clouded with concern.

Natalie shook her head. Her face was supposed to be red with rage, not pale. She had not been able to speak for herself, and it was disgraceful. She tried to quickly compose herself, and her eyes found the ballerina her cousin held. "Where did you find that?"

Hannah smiled. "The puppet player asked us some questions. I answered correctly, earning this pretty ballerina." Then she frowned. "Are you certain you are well, Natalie?"

Natalie managed a faint smile and a nod before taking her cousin's arm. She could see that Hannah wanted to ask again but she refused to give her the chance, glad she had not been present to witness her humiliation.

They continued walking along the Serpentine and after a while, Hannah looked up. "Do you think it will rain soon?"

Following her eyes, Natalie saw the sky was completely overcast. "Yes, and we should go." The impending storm gave Natalie an excuse to leave the park. They walked back to the waiting carriage, and about twenty minutes later, they arrived at Clifford House in Berkeley Square.

Natalie went up to her bedchamber while Hannah sought George, and as soon as she closed the door behind her, she leaned against it, fighting every painful memory she had worked for years to keep down.

It took one encounter with Jasper to unleash them, and they pressed against the back of her eyes, causing them to sting. She furiously blinked away the tears blurring her vision, rage tightening her chest, and moved to her writing desk by the window. Natalie sat and opened a drawer, removing a folded piece of parchment that had been there for more than two years.

The paper contained a list of everything she wanted to do in her lifetime but never had the opportunity. All of those things were daring and demanded courage that she did not possess. Her situation was not likely going to change, and perhaps it was time to step out from the shadows and live as she truly wanted to.

Unfolding the list, she began to read:

Kiss a rake

Kiss a proper gentleman

Swim in the Serpentine

Slip away with a gentleman during a ball

Wear a scandalous dress

Gamble in a gentlemen's club

Smoke cheroot and drink until I lose my mind and balance

Fence

Ask a gentleman to dance

Be truly wanted. Loved.

Picking up a quill and dipping it in ink, Natalie added one more item to the list:

Ruin Jasper's reputation.

Chapter Two

Shameless men have come forward with the claims of being the Masked Rogue without proof. We are offering a reward for whoever can reveal his face to society —The Londoner.

Natalie wanted him to feel the pain she had lived with for nine years. Certainly, it would be much more difficult to ruin a man's reputation, and he was known in society as a perfect duke.

Her task would be tough, but she was willing to do what it took. If he had truly forgotten what he had done to her, then she would gladly remind him.

A knock came at her door as she finished writing on her list. She quickly wiped her tears with the pad of her fingers and put the list away, rising. "Yes?"

"May I come in?" Hannah asked.

Smoothing her hands down her blue muslin dress, she called for her cousin to enter. Hannah immediately frowned when she walked in and looked at Natalie.

"Is something the matter, Natalie?" she asked. "You were very quiet on our ride back. Did something happen?"

Natalie shook her head. "I am well, Hannah. You must not worry about me."

Hannah still looked skeptical despite that answer, but she said. "You should rest before dinner."

"Yes, I will do that."

Her cousin regarded her as though she wished to say more, but she nodded and left. Natalie allowed a deep sigh. A walk would calm her, but she was unwilling to leave the house at this time because her fears had been revived. She felt as though a crowd would be waiting in front of the house to launch hurtful words at her.

She picked up a basket with her sewing and weaving items and sat like a monk on her bed. Ladies did not trade, but Natalie did in secret to help her family. She made bonnets and dresses and sold them to her friend Mary Lynch, who was a modiste with a shop on Bond Street.

Ladies loved Mary's shop, so naturally, they believed some of the bonnets and dresses she displayed were of her making, which was convenient for Natalie.

She had no siblings, her mother died an hour after her birth, and her father passed away five years ago. Hannah and George were all she had, and poor George inherited her father's debts, which Jasper caused. What she did helped, and it also gave her a sense of purpose in the world.

"Shall I read now?" Hannah asked, raising the sheet she had just finished writing on as they waited in the drawing room for dinner to be announced.

"Yes," George replied, while Natalie straightened in her seat. Hannah wrote anonymously for The Londoner, and her articles were solely about the Masked Rogue of London. The money she earned from that was her contribution to the family, and she always read the pieces she wrote to George and Natalie before submitting them for publication.

She was two-and-twenty and seeking a husband. Until she found one, she too felt obligated to help George in any way she could.

Clearing her throat, Hannah began, "*Lord Mansfield had the misfortune of losing a wager last night against the Masked Rogue. Now the exact sum is unknown because the Baron would not reveal it, but it is large enough that he might part with a property...*"

"From whom do you hear what to report?" George asked.

"Oh, I cannot tell you that, Brother," Hannah laughed. They had been asking her that question for a while and she refused to tell. Hannah was still far from finding the rogue's identity, but she had managed to become thoroughly informed about where he went and what he did.

Now, Natalie wondered how much fortune he had amassed over the years through his wagers—and he won nearly everyone he made. "Does he truly favor women with red hair?" she asked.

"Yes, he does. Nearly every woman in his company has red hair or is wearing a red wig."

George turned to look at Natalie, consternation widening his green eyes. A blush crept up her cheeks. "I am not asking because I have red hair, George," she mumbled. "I am merely as curious as the *ton* is about him."

"Well..." he cleared his throat, "we do not know if he is a gentleman. He certainly has the comportment of one but any scoundrel could pretend to be a gentleman, especially one behind a mask."

Natalie's thoughts veered onto a path that made her blush even though she had never seen the Masked Rogue. Blinking, she shifted in her seat and composed herself. Should she try to find him with her cousin's help? She was no longer concerned about her reputation, and she could add a wish to her list. *Find the Masked Rogue.*

She was not sure what she would do if she found him but a kiss would be a good start. *Yes, I should do this.*

"I have yet to find where he lives," Hannah complained, folding the sheet and sealing it.

"Why do you want to know where he lives?" Natalie asked, leaning slightly forward, which drew George's attention and he cleared his throat. He had always been very protective of both Natalie and his sister.

"Why, I would be closer to finding his face once I have his address."

The butler appeared in the doorway and George stood, saying, "I wish you luck, Sister."

He offered Natalie his arm, and they moved to the dining room for dinner. As they began to eat, she noticed a change in George's demeanor. "Is something the matter?"

His hesitation told her that it was about money. She disliked such discussions, and she should have grown accustomed to them by now, but she took a sip of her wine to prepare herself before asking, "What do you wish to talk about, George?"

"We need to further reduce our expenses," he replied, looking dolefully from Natalie to Hannah.

"Lady Barton invited us to her autumn ball," Hannah said, "but we do not have to attend, and if we must, then we will not have new dresses made. We shall wear one of our old ones."

They were rarely invited to balls—even during the social season—and they were excited when they received an invitation last week. They planned to have new dresses because most of the ones they had were out of fashion. Natalie could make them new dresses, but they had wanted a proper modiste to do it so they could truly feel like they were part of the *ton*. The illusion of privilege was sometimes a salve for their wounds.

"Yes, I agree with Hannah," Natalie said. "I can alter our old dresses and no one will know."

George sighed, suddenly looking older than his age of two-and-thirty. He contemplated their suggestion for a moment before shaking his head. "No. My sisters shall have new dresses. They might not be the same as what you are accustomed to but you will have something new, nevertheless. Besides, the price of a dress is not very significant." He smiled to brighten the place, and although they returned the gesture, the air remained heavy with the burdens on the family.

Hannah made to object, but Natalie stopped her with a look. "What else can we do?" It was evident that George was already feeling as though he had failed them. The best they could do for him was to accept what he was giving them. She silently promised to work harder to replace what they would spend on the new dresses.

"We have to dismiss some of the household. A maid or two should make a difference," he suggested, "or we could reduce their wages."

Natalie gently placed a hand on his arm. "It is better to dismiss them. We can give them good references that will enable them to find better situations."

"Yes, you are correct. I would be lost without you two." He gave them an appreciative smile. "Thank you."

"What is the purpose of family if not to look after one another." She took his hand, then frowned when she noticed, for the first time, how lean his fingers had become. George's health suffered greatly for how much he exerted himself in his attempts to repay their debts and provide for them. He hid it well from them, but it was at times like this that Natalie noticed.

Guilt clenched her gut as she recalled the cause of it all. Oliver Bargrave had pronounced Jasper's prank a scandal, and he came to her father and collected money from him for his silence. Months later,

Oliver forced her father to give him a large part of his coal mining business using the scandal as leverage. Too afraid to have his daughter's reputation ruined, her father agreed, and fell into debt trying to revive his remaining fortune.

The scandal remained hidden but the price was too much. As a result of their lost fortune, gentlemen avoided Natalie because she had no dowry, and when she reached the age of five-and-twenty, she was deemed a spinster.

George still owned a portion of the business but it was a very small one. Not once had Natalie's father or George ever blamed her for what had happened, nor had they shown their displeasure in any way. She was immensely grateful to them, but her gratitude did nothing to assuage her guilt.

After dinner, George went to his study, while Hannah moved to the library to read. Left alone, Natalie decided to retire early. Within the walls of her room, the day's events rattled in her thoughts.

Jasper will surely pay for what he had done to her family, but before then, she had a task she could complete with him. *Kiss a proper gentleman.* He was a perfect man in society's eyes, thus, he qualified.

She rose from her chair in front of the hearth and walked to her vanity, assessing her appearance. Her pale blue lace dress complimented her red hair and gave her hazel eyes a green hue. Yes, she will kiss a proper gentleman tonight before she lost the unexpected courage she had gained.

Removing a black cloak from a rack and throwing it over her shoulders, she picked up her gloves and reticule, and she slipped out of her bedchamber, moving as quietly as she could. Her heart beat faster, and her eyes darted in every direction. She had never snuck out of the house before, and if George found her, not only would he prevent her from leaving but he would worry.

He also would never understand her list, especially because he still hoped she would find a good gentleman and marry. She descended the stairs and hurried toward the rear of the house where the servants' entrance was located. Natalie opened it as quietly as she could and stepped out, closing it behind her.

She took a deep breath and walked down the alley to the street where she hired a hack, giving the driver Jasper's address, a few miles outside the city of Westminster.

As she settled in the carriage and flutters threatened to make her run back to the safety of Clifford House, she swallowed and took another steadying breath.

Tonight, the course of my life changes. I will not quail, she vowed.

Chapter Three

We have it on good authority that the Masked Rogue is a very sad man. A demimonde, whose name we shan't reveal, claimed to have seen grief in his gaze during an encounter. Many others have pronounced the same, and we believe that there is some truth to this tale.

Jasper opened the middle drawer of his desk, but instead of picking up the ledger he intended to retrieve, his hand found a black mask. He removed it and stared at it for a while, thinking.

He was the fifth Duke of Amsthorne, and like the last two before him, he was going to die in months. This mask had given him the chance to live as he pleased before their family curse would come to claim him. It saved him from tainting his family's pristine reputation.

Jasper sighed as he continued to stare at the mask, realizing that he was lying to himself at this very moment. He was a coward who hid behind the Masked Rogue instead of living truthfully. He feared death, and that ought to have encouraged honesty. Now all of London—nay, England—wanted him.

That and the darkness of his curse shadowed every step he took, occupied every space in his thoughts, and consumed his dreams at night. His father and grandfather died at five-and-thirty from mysterious illnesses, and he was sure the same would happen to him. Jasper shut his eyes and ground his teeth, his heart aching anew. Dwelling upon this issue never did him well, and it would not suddenly whim to serve him. He must continue on the path he was on. Live the rest of his days as he pleased so he would die knowing he controlled what he could.

Placing the mask back in the drawer, he retrieved the ledger and set it atop his desk before gaining his feet, walking to a table by a bookshelf, and picking up a brandy decanter. A knock came as he was pouring a finger of brandy into a glass.

"Come in," he called, walking back to his desk with his liquor. His aunt, Lady Phoebe Dawson, walked into the room, her dark eyebrows contracting when she saw the glass between his fingers. She never liked it when he drank. She also did not believe the curse.

"Should I have some tea brought in for you?" she asked, coming to sit in the chair before his desk.

"You would do anything to take my brandy away, would you not?" Jasper intoned. Phoebe was the only mother he had ever known. She was his late mother's sister, and at the time of her passing, she made Phoebe promise to look after Jasper. Or so he was told.

"Quite so," she replied, placing what looked like invitations on his desk. "Lady Barton invited us to her autumn ball. I am hoping you would attend…" she raised one dark eyebrow, "with Miss Gilmore."

Jasper's eyes rolled. The only reason he was paying Miss Gilmore any attention was because of his image as a duke, and to please his aunt. She had chosen her for him to court, and he obliged because he did not have long to live, and her happiness was important to him.

"Must I?" he asked, the corner of his mouth curving upward in jest.

"Yes, Jasper. Miss Gilmore is a very good young lady. She has the qualities to become a duchess."

No, she does not, he was tempted to argue. Miss Gilmore was an arrogant chit without an inkling about how harsh life could be. He had been disgusted with her treatment of Lady Natalie, who was higher in rank, and appeared to be older, too. He had never seen her behave thusly before, but then she thought he was too far away to hear what she said.

Poor Lady Natalie had ostensibly been too surprised to defend herself, and he was happy to step in as her champion. She was also a delight to look at.

The Londoner was right about his tastes in women. Red hair roused his passion, and many of the demimondaines he knew wore red wigs to please him. He never asked them to, but he had a jolly when they did.

Lady Natalie was natural, and he wondered what she was like, and if he could find her. No, the proper question was if she would be willing to have his company. He would rather spend his days pretending to court *her* instead of Miss Gilmore.

"Jasper?"

His aunt's voice interrupted his thoughts, and he looked up. "Hmm?"

"I asked if you would attend."

Jasper nodded. He did not want to argue, and the more the days passed, the more he yearned for peace. He could never have internal peace, but he could have some in his household.

"I also think it is time you make your intentions towards Alexandra known in society," Phoebe continued. "You should consider marrying her."

Jasper immediately raised a hand to stop her. "You know I cannot do that."

His aunt blinked. "Is this because of that silly curse?" Before he could respond, she continued with, "You would be happier if you removed that notion from your mind. There is no curse in this family, and that is all I am saying about that this evening."

Phoebe had not been present when his father died. She did not see what Jasper had, and what had ultimately convinced him that this was a curse. She would never understand how selfish and cruel he would be if he married; to leave a young widow, and perhaps a child who would never know him, would plague his afterlife for eternity.

"I shall give it some thought," he murmured to placate her, and after studying his face for a moment, she believed him.

"I saw the butler coming to give you a letter but I took it from him." She set down a missive atop the invitations. One glance at the crest on the seal, and Jasper grinned.

It was from his dearest friend, Oliver Bargrave, the Earl of Ecklehill. Oliver had been journeying about the world for the past two years, and his letters were as rare as they were appreciated.

When he picked up the letter, his aunt decided to leave. She walked to the door, but before she opened it, she turned and said over her shoulder, "Miss Gilmore and I will be shopping tomorrow afternoon. You may promenade with her if you wish."

"Yes," Jasper said, opening the letter. "Goodnight Aunt Phoebe." He heard her chuckle as she left. Shaking his head slightly, he read:

Amsthorne,

I have excellent news, my friend! By the time you read this letter, I will be on a ship bound for England. I hope to return before the snow settles.

I shall keep this letter short because I have much to tell you when I return. I hope you are not planning to marry yet, for I wish to be reacquainted with society. Who better to help me with that?

Sincerely,

Lord Ecklehill

. . .

Jasper smiled as he folded the letter. Oliver would return in time for his thirty-fifth birthday, and he will have the chance to bid him a proper farewell. Another knock sounded at his door and when he answered, his butler, Wayne, walked in.

"There is a caller for you, Your Grace."

"Who is it?"

"A lady, Your Grace, but she would not give her name."

Jasper glanced at the small clock on his desk. It was past ten and raining. What would a lady be doing in his manor at this time? "Are you certain she did not call upon my aunt?"

"I am, Your Grace. She specifically asked for an audience with you. She is in the drawing room."

Surprised and curious, Jasper stood to find out who this lady was and what she wanted from him.

Chapter Four

Ladies of the ton, should you find yourself in close proximity with the Masked Rogue, even in a crowded place, leave as soon as you can, and keep your gaze lowered. A glance from that scoundrel could smother your honor.

Natalie anxiously wrung the skirt of her dress between her fingers, unable to slow the rapid beating of her heart. She had come to ask Jasper to kiss her, or seduce him if she must, but she was close to fleeing before he even joined her.

Her stomach clenched when she heard strong footfalls outside the drawing room. Moving to the edge of the chair she was sitting in, she allowed a shaky breath and closed her eyes, seeking strength from within. Revenge was certainly more difficult than she ever anticipated.

Jasper appeared in the doorway, and his dark brows rose the instant he saw her. "Lady Natalie?"

She wondered for how long he would continue to pretend to forget. She still did not believe that he had no recollection of that night. She rose slowly from her chair and held her hands in front of her, curtsying.

"Is something the matter?" he asked as he walked further into the room. He looked earnestly concerned but she knew not to believe everything she saw.

"Your Grace, I apologize for the sudden visit." Natalie forced a smile, while his eyes moved appreciatively over her. Beneath it all, she found it challenging to read him, and she felt she was in a disadvantageous position as a result.

Natalie apologized for the late-night call, trying not to notice how his gaze roamed over her almost in appraisal. Beneath the concern, his expression was inscrutable, and Natalie wished she could read him.

He gestured for her to sit. "Are you accompanied by anyone?" Natalie had almost forgotten how proper he was. She did not know how he kept a perfect image, even in the confines of his own manor.

"No, I came alone," she replied as she sat, and his brows ascended higher.

"May I ask why you would come to an unmarried Duke's residence without a chaperone?"

She took a breath. "A chaperone should never be present for what I am here for."

Jasper inclined his head, and his eyes gleamed with interest at her suggestion even though he had yet to learn its nature. Then his gaze seemed to darken as it slid from her face, down her neck, and rested on her bosom. Heat coated her skin, and her mouth dried suddenly.

"Then what are you here for, My Lady?" he asked, his gaze returning to her eyes.

The image of him rejecting her, and asking her to leave his home played in her mind, and her resolve faltered. Her desire to fulfill her aspirations countered her fears, however. "I came to kiss you, Your Grace." Her shoulders were straight, and her chin was high as she spoke. There was a confidence in her voice that she had never heard before.

Jasper blinked slowly, and Natalie held her breath. "I beg your pardon?"

"I am sure you heard me clearly, Your Grace, but if I must repeat myself, then—"

"Why do you want me to kiss you?" he asked, leaning forward in his seat and resting his elbows on his thighs. There was a hint of a smile on his features that suggested he would not throw her out as she feared.

"I am here to kiss *you*," she corrected him, and a wide grin spread over his face.

"I do not know why you want to kiss me, but whatever your reason is, my answer is yes."

A flutter began in the pit of her belly, and she sounded breathless when she spoke. "You...agree?"

Jasper grinned. "A lovely woman offering me a kiss? How could I refuse?"

She lowered her eyes as a deep blush crept onto her cheeks. He stood and offered his hand. She did not know what he was planning to do, but she placed her hand in his and allowed him to draw her to her feet.

"Shall we finish this discussion in my study?"

Now a shiver ran through her. "Yes," she replied, and he led her out of the drawing room. There was no one in the front hall or any of the hallways, but she was not surprised, given the hour.

The manor was incredibly beautiful with baroque designs that made her feel as though she was in a French palace—though she had never been to France. They walked through an archway beyond a grand staircase, then down a hallway with only one door along its length. Jasper opened it and gestured for her to precede him into the room.

The first thing to greet her as she walked into the study was the scent of brandy, leather, and wood. Her senses were luxuriously pleased, and when he entered and closed the door, she knew he was looking at her.

The heat from his gaze moved down her body in delicious waves to settle in her core.

"You wish to kiss me, yet you have your back to me," he murmured, and she realized he was closer than she thought.

Natalie turned around, her heart pounding, and her knees softening. His expression told her he was amused, and it also reminded her that she had not the slightest inkling of what to do. Relying on her instincts, she moved closer to him and placed her hands on his broad shoulders. His mouth curved, and she closed her eyes, rising on the tips of her toes.

Their lips touched, and Jasper cupped her cheek with one hand, while the other circled her waist. He parted his lips for her, sweetly guiding her through it. Slowly, he deepened the kiss and pulled her closer, filling her body with pulses of need. He loosened her cloak, and it fell to the floor. Natalie had not expected to feel such passion from something as simple as a kiss.

This was not merely a kiss, however. It was more, with old and hidden emotions involved. She had once yearned to be in his arms, and he betrayed her. The yearning was still present, but the way he was holding her and gliding his tongue along hers was telling of his own desire, and it made her feel powerful.

She raked her fingers through his hair, and he groaned, pressing her into his hardening body. A moan slipped past her lips when he kissed her neck. "Your Grace," she breathed.

"Yes?" His mouth moved to the mounds of her breasts, and she sighed, arching her back. Her sex throbbed with want, and her nipples perked beneath her dress.

"Is this...part of the kiss?" she asked.

Jasper hooked a finger into the neckline of her dress and pulled it down slightly, tasting her skin and murmuring, "A kiss could be so much more."

Natalie wondered how much more, and she wished to discover it, but she began to pull away from him. She had gotten what she came for, and although her body was begging her to ask him for more, she could not. He straightened, and traced the line of her jaw with his forefinger, his eyes on her lips.

"Are you satisfied, Lady Natalie?" he asked, and she hesitated in her response, leading him to add, "I will be happy to let you have another."

Natalie sucked in her breath to keep herself from agreeing. No matter what, he was still the man who tore her heart into pieces years ago. "Thank you, Your Grace, but one kiss is quite enough."

"Are you certain?" He quirked a brow, and she nodded, stepping away from him.

"Yes, I am."

He regarded her for a while longer, and even though she could not interpret the look in his eyes, her skin continued to warm. "Very well," he said at length. "Would you like some wine?"

"No, thank you. I should leave."

"Did you come with your carriage?" he asked, retrieving her cloak from the floor and handing it to her.

"No, a hackney brought me."

"Then allow me to arrange for my carriage to take you home."

Natalie nodded, and he turned and exited the room. She lowered herself into the chair closest to her and held her cloak up to her chest. He was being kind to her, and she could not understand it as she was torn between appreciation and distrust.

She looked around the study and wondered why he was still unmarried. He should be five-and-thirty, and most Dukes were already married at his age to ensure the continuity of their bloodlines. Perhaps he had no need for a wife. Or was something preventing him?

I am giving this too much thought, she told herself. Besides, she had to think of a way to ruin his reputation. Natalie had a thought, and she rose, approaching the large desk. Everyone had secrets, and if she could find Jasper's, then all she would have to do was give the information to The Londoner through Hannah.

She glanced behind her to ensure the door was closed. Several correspondences lay on his desk, and as she was reaching for the closest to her, footsteps sounded beyond the door. Her heart skipped, and she ran back to her seat, holding herself stiffly as Jasper returned.

"The carriage has been prepared," he said.

Natalie stood and wore her cloak before adjusting her gloves and looking up at him. "I thank you, Your Grace." She curtsied.

"It was my pleasure," he returned, his eyes glinting with even more interest. "You need not worry about your reputation. I will ensure it is protected."

"I have no care for my reputation," Natalie blurted, then sucked in her lips. She truly did not care for her reputation, but she had to be proper because Hannah was on the marriage mart, and a scandal could ruin her chances of making a good match, or any match at all.

Jasper chuckled. "Yet you refused to give the butler your name."

"Caution will always serve a man," she retorted.

"Indeed." He held out a hand, and when she placed her fingers on his palm, he kissed her knuckles. Another fiery jolt ran through her, and she bit the insides of her cheeks.

He led her out of the study and through hallways to a door on the side of the manor. A carriage was waiting with a driver and a footman. Again, Natalie was caught between gratitude and vengeance.

"Good night," she said, wishing to hurriedly leave him. The longer she stayed, the more she found his good gestures confounding.

"Be well, My Lady," he whispered, kissing her hand again. Then he handed her into the carriage.

As it pulled away, Natalie sighed with both relief and anguish. She was certain she would never find peace until she avenged the spirit of her youth.

Chapter Five

The Masked Rogue of London might not be residing in London. We ought to have found his home if he were. Ladies and gentlemen, we will be moving our search outside of town. The reward for his face has been doubled.

Thoughts of her kiss with Jasper plagued Natalie over breakfast such that she barely touched her food. Hannah also occasionally glanced at her, while George's attention appeared to be on the correspondences he was reading.

No one was aware of where she had been the night before, and she had slipped back into the house and her bedchamber with as much ease as she had when leaving. Sleep had been challenging, however, because she had been planning. She would need Hannah's help to find what to fulfill her eleventh wish with; *Ruin Jasper's reputation.*

George shot up suddenly, and Natalie's eyes snapped to his face. He was glaring at the missive in his hand, and his pallor was consternating. "What happened?" she asked.

He seemed to only just recall their presence, and he fell back and sat straighter in his chair, clearing his throat. "It is nothing you need to concern yourselves with," he reassured them, but Natalie knew his composure was contrived. Something was wrong. She could see it in the lines around the corners of his mouth. He drank the last drops of his tea and rose. "I will be in my study."

Natalie and Hannah looked at each other after he had left. "What can we do to help him?" her cousin asked, her eyes misting. This was not the first time they were witnessing such outbursts, and they always felt helpless.

"I will speak to him," Natalie replied, gaining her feet. She wanted George to know that whatever it was, they could overcome it together as a family. Hannah nodded as she left the breakfast room.

Natalie knocked gently on his study door, and at his response, she opened the door and stepped inside. George was hunched over a ledger, and his spectacles were slowly slipping down his nose. He had excellent sight before he became Earl, but after spending long nights poring over the accounts, he had to have his eyes examined and spectacles prescribed.

"Natalie," he said when he looked up, "I hope you did not come here because you are worried about me."

"That is exactly why I am here," she said, sitting in one of the chairs by the hearth. It was very cold in London now, and it would be even colder once winter arrived. They only heated the rooms they used, which were only about three rooms—excluding their bed chambers and the servants' rooms. "What happened, George?" Natalie asked.

He passed a hand over his brow before picking up a letter and walking up to her. "This arrived last night but I did not get the chance to read it until this morning."

She saw the Earl of Ecklehill's crest on the broken seal, and her stomach turned. Oliver had been traveling for the last two years, and they had only needed to communicate with his solicitors. His return could mean more demands from him that would plunge them further into debt. She almost gave the letter back to George, telling him she understood, but she had to read it. She had to be brave.

CLIFFORD,

I hope this letter finds you and your family well. I will be returning to England this winter. I have a new business proposition for you, one I hope you will accept. We shall discuss it when I return.

Sincerely,

Lord Ecklehill

ENQUIRING ABOUT THEIR WELL-BEING WAS ABSOLUTE MOCKERY, AND Natalie's jaw clenched. "Do you know what the proposition might be?" she asked George, giving the letter back to him.

He shook his head. "I wish I did so that I may prepare for it, whatever it is." She could see that he was not expecting anything good, and they all had a good reason for such low expectations.

Seeing how the news of Oliver's impending return troubled her, George took her hand and squeezed it. "I will not allow him to harm you," he said. Oliver could use her reputation to take the little they had left away from them, and that was her greatest fear now.

"Thank you, George, for all that you do for us." She smiled up at him, wishing she could do more to comfort him.

"You do not have to thank me, Natalie. You are as much my sister as Hannah, and we are all we have."

She hugged him, her chest tight and heavy. "Everything will be well for us again," she murmured.

"Yes, it will."

Natalie left him several minutes later and went up to her bedchamber to gather the dresses and bonnets she was going to take to Mary this afternoon. When she entered the room, she found that Hannah had already placed the two bonnets in a box and was folding the dresses.

"I thought you would need some help," she said.

"I do, Hannah. It is very thoughtful of you."

"Did George tell you what happened?"

"Oliver is returning to town."

Hannah's eyes widened. "So soon?"

"He has been gone for two years." Natalie picked up the other dress and began to fold it.

"That vile blackguard could never be gone for long enough, Natalie."

"I know. I only hope he will not trouble us." Natalie did not tell Hannah about the proposition because she did not want her to worry. "We should go to Mary's shop now."

They finished folding the dresses and placed them in a valise, before having one of the only two footmen in their employ carry them to the carriage. Then they rode to Mary's shop.

As they did every time, the footman carried the bonnets and dresses in through the entrance on the side of the shop, while Natalie and Hannah walked in through the front door. This way, no one suspected what they were truly there for. Most times, Mary collected the things herself but she had been quite occupied as of late.

Mary peeked from behind the skirt of the lady whose measurements she was taking and clapped her hands in delight. "Oh, Lady Natalie! How wonderful to see you."

The lady turned and looked Natalie over. Seemingly unimpressed, she sniffed and turned. Natalie was not unaccustomed to such treatment. Society did not pity her because she was a spinster. No, they disliked her outright, and they did not hesitate to show it.

Natalie and Hannah sat to wait for the lady to leave, and a roll of ivory satin caught her attention. It shimmered in the late-morning light, and Natalie thought it would make a splendid dress. Some minutes later, the door opened and Alexandra walked in with Lady Phoebe Dawson, Jasper's aunt. Natalie's stomach flipped at the sight of them, and she kept her gaze down.

First, because she had kissed Jasper the night before in his manor, where his aunt lived, and second, because she did not want trouble with Alexandra. Of course, Natalie had no say in the latter, for the moment Alexandra saw her, she tapped Lady Phoebe's shoulder and pointed at her.

"My Lady, allow me to introduce a *dear* friend of mine, Lady Natalie Reeves." The condescension in Alexandra's tone was all but apparent.

Lady Phoebe smiled pleasantly as Natalie stood and curtsied. "It is a pleasure to make your acquaintance, Lady Natalie." Alexandra's eyes narrowed. She likely had not expected Lady Phoebe to be this cordial.

"It is my pleasure, as well, My Lady." Natalie turned to Hannah. "This is my cousin, Miss Hannah Reeves."

Something sparked in Lady Phoebe's blue eyes. "You look quite familiar, Miss Reeves. Have we met before?"

Hannah smiled demurely and lowered her eyes. "Yes, My Lady. I found your lost reticule at Lady Miller's ball in spring."

Natalie recalled the incident but she did not know it was Lady Phoebe because she had not attended that particular ball due to a cold.

"Oh, that is true!" Lady Phoebe laughed. "How wonderful to see you again, and know your name."

Natalie looked at Alexandra to find her wearing a disappointed expression. As soon as the lady Mary was attending to left, she moved to have her measurements taken. Natalie suspected Alexandra did that to keep her displeasure hidden. After all, she pretended to have a good character in public.

"Lady Natalie, that is quite a fine dress you are wearing," Lady Phoebe complimented, surprising her.

She had made the pale green muslin dress herself. Deciding to take the opportunity she had been presented, she said, "Thank you, My Lady. Miss Lynch made it for me."

Lady Phoebe turned to Mary with a bright smile. "I would like to have every dress I order today in this style."

Natalie and Mary exchanged a look. This meant that Natalie would sew the dresses, and her family would have more money. She was very fortunate to have met Lady Phoebe today, and she supposed she should silently thank Alexandra for the introduction.

"Yes, My Lady," Mary replied. "Lady Natalie gave me the idea for the style. She was very specific about what she wanted."

"Oh? We should have tea sometime, Lady Natalie," Lady Phoebe said, surprising her yet again. "I would like to hear all about your remarkable taste. My former modiste disappointed me thoroughly, you see, and Miss Lynch was a very good recommendation. I did not know she had a muse."

"Tea would be splendid, My Lady," Natalie responded, hope swelling in her heart. Perhaps Lady Phoebe would do her good in many ways even though she was Jasper's aunt.

They had a pleasant conversation, and when it was time to leave, Natalie decided that she would send for the ivory satin later. She did not know what she would do with it but it beckoned to her, making her dearly wish to have it in her possession.

NATALIE WAS UNABLE TO SLEEP THAT EVENING, AS THOUGHTS OF Jasper ran through her mind. Lady Phoebe had invited them to tea, and although the day had not been chosen, she was nervous about the possibility of seeing him again.

She sat up and ran her hand through her hair. She could accomplish another aspiration on her list to keep herself distracted. Now that she had embarked on this journey, she did not want to stop. Leaving the bed, she dressed in a simple brown dress and pulled her heavy wool cloak around her shoulders.

Then she left the house the same way she did the night before, giving the hack driver directions to Hyde Park. A lady should never be alone in a park after sundown. In fact, she should never be out alone at any other time, but Natalie barely considered herself a lady. Midnight was upon her, and her sense of adventure was dominating her reasoning.

She drew the hood of her cloak over her eyes after disembarking at the park and began to walk down the deserted paths, the lamps, which were few and far between—her only source of illumination. The quietness was peaceful, and somehow, Natalie was not afraid.

Finding the Serpentine, she walked east along the bank until she reached where the foliage was thickest. Moving behind a bush, she removed her cloak, shivering when the cold night air touched her skin. She could freeze out here, and she was sure the water was colder. But she was already here, and she would not fail by quailing.

Natalie unfastened the buttons of her dress, and as she was about to pull it down, rustling from a bush nearby reached her ears, and she stiffened. Her heart began to pound, and she told herself that it was a rodent or some other creature.

But rodents should be in hibernation at this time of the year, and the thought sent a chill down her back, while her skin crawled with fear. She peered at the darkness but saw no one.

"Well, well," a voice said behind her, and she jumped, turning around, "what have we here?" A man stepped out from behind the bush, and another followed him.

Chapter Six

The Masked Rogue is not in possession of a heart. Poor Lord Mansfield has nothing left. The Rogue took everything, and he even had the impudence to ask him to offer his daughter to settle the remainder of the debts. What a deplorable man! Fortunately, Lord Mansfield does not have a daughter.

"Who is this?" One of the sots asked as he walked toward Natalie. She held her dress up, and her eyes were bulging with fear. She looked around for help but there was no one around.

"A pretty little dove all alone at night?" Another foxed scoundrel slurred.

Natalie quickly picked up her cloak but someone snatched it from her. She did not wait to see who, or even fight, and she turned to flee. Her wrist was grabbed, and when her eyes found the man holding her, she realized with burning terror that there were three of them.

Lord, help me! she prayed, regretting coming here at this hour.

"If you are going for a swim, we'd like to join." The man holding her wrist pushed her forward and into the arms of another. Natalie struggled against him, and when his hold was too firm, she screamed.

He clapped a hand over her mouth and squeezed her jaw, stings of curses pouring from him. Still, she kicked and fought, because no one would help her. Natalie had brought herself into this hell, and she was her only hope of escape. With her elbows and heels, she did all she could to free herself, her tears blinding her, but the men laughed, seemingly enjoying her torment.

"You filthy bastards!" someone growled, and Natalie was suddenly released. A cloaked figure planted the man holding her a facer, and the remaining two moved to fight him, but they stood to assess the situation before attacking. Paying them no attention, her rescuer threw the man onto the ground and kicked him.

Natalie scrambled backward, staring with wide eyes. The second man fled, while the third, in a show of strength, grabbed her rescuer's cloak. He turned around and a gasp escaped her at the sight of his face.

The man who had come to her defense was none other than the Masked Rogue. She had never seen him before but she knew enough to recognize him. He wore a white mask tonight, which enabled her to see him in the darkness. He caught her second attacker by the lapels of his coat and punched his face. His strength was impressive, and his movement transfixed her.

A hand circled her arm, and she was yanked backward. As she was spun around, she saw the third man, whom she thought had fled. "You will pay for this, you little harlot!"

Before she could understand what was happening, Natalie was carried and thrown into the freezing Serpentine. She flailed and kicked under the water until she broke the surface, gasping and coughing.

A deafening sound rent the air, and in that fraction of a second, she felt nothing, not even the cold, biting and numbing her limbs. Then she blinked as she saw the men running. When the rogue turned to face her, she found a pistol in his hand.

Cursing, he threw the pistol and removed his cloak before jumping into the water. His arms came around her, and she began to struggle again. Natalie knew he was attempting to help her but she was still afraid. He could easily have driven the sots away so he could have her for himself.

"Damn it, woman!" he cursed, his arms tightening around her waist, "I am helping you!"

"No!" Natalie yelled, blindly shoving a hand in the direction of his face. "I can swim. I can save myself!" Once she caught something, she pulled. He released her immediately and she looked down to see that she was holding his mask. She glanced up quickly, and he turned away. Not before she saw his face, however.

"Jasper?" she gasped, frozen again.

"Natalie?" He sounded as though he was in disbelief. He seemed to be seeing her for the first time since this horrid night began. "Bloody hell!"

His arms came around her waist again and he pulled her to him. She did not fight him this time. Either shock had robbed her of her will to fight or the familiarity between them was preventing her; she was not sure which was it. He swam to the bank and carried her out of the water.

Jasper took her shoulders and leaned until their eyes were at the same level. She could not properly read his expression in the darkness but she could tell he was angry. "What are you doing here?"

"You...you are the rogue," she whispered, still in disbelief.

"It does not matter what I am," he growled, taking his mask from her and covering his face again. "What are you doing here alone at this hour?"

That seemed to bring her back to reality, and she blinked several times, pushing her damp hair from her face and shivering. "I...I came to swim."

He stared at her as though she had gone mad. "Do you know how cold it is?"

"Of course, I do!" Her teeth chattered to push her point. "But I could scarcely do so in the afternoon!"

Jasper picked up his dry cloak and wrapped it around her, and she almost sighed from the warmth. It was lined with fur. "I will not pretend to understand the reason you thought it a good idea to swim in the river, but I am returning you home."

"You are?" She looked up at him, confused.

He said nothing as he retrieved his pistol and slipped it into his coat pocket. Still silent, he gathered her cloak and took her hand.

⁂

WHEN JASPER DECIDED TO TAKE A WALK IN THE PARK, HE NEVER imagined he would have to rescue a woman from reprobates, and Lady Natalie no less. He had never really seen her before, but after the incident at Hyde park, he had seen her two more times, and in the space of three days!

He was angry with her for placing herself in such a position, and the thought of what could have happened to her had he not heard her scream wrenched his gut. Jasper glanced at her as they neared a lamp.

She was still shivering, and her pale face made him soften. He slowed and turned her to face him. "Why?" he asked again, wanting to know why she would come out at midnight to swim.

"I wanted to," she replied. Her eyes gleamed like ambers, and he swallowed. He was cold but she was making his body defy nature by arousing him. Her wet dress had clung enticingly to her body, and the sight was one of the reasons he covered her with his cloak.

"Was there a specific reason?"

"Well, it is something I wished to do before I die." The last word twisted something in his chest, and he wondered if she was trying to fulfill her desires because death loomed over her. After all, she had come to kiss him last night. It was no coincidence that he found her here tonight.

"Very well." He turned and continued walking with her hand still in his.

They approached the horse he had tied by a tree to graze, and she asked, "Is that yours?"

"Yes." Jasper slowed, watching her fine eyebrows furrow. "Is something wrong?"

"Are we riding together?"

Jasper felt the corner of his mouth curve. "I do not see a better way to take you home. Does riding with me trouble you?"

"I...well..."

He leaned close to her. "If you could allow me to kiss you, then surely, you should not mind sharing a saddle with me."

He could not tell whether or not she blushed but she caught her lower lip between her teeth, and his body reacted. More specifically, his groin became engorged. He had not been able to forget their kiss, and upon waking this morning, he had thought—more than any sane man should—of seeing her again.

"I did not allow you to kiss me," she returned fiercely. "*I* kissed *you*."

"Yes, of course. Pardon my error."

That seemed to vex her further. "Do not condescend to me." She pulled her hand from his and marched to the horse. She was doing it again, and it confused him.

Last night, Jasper saw what he thought was disdain in her eyes but it did not stay long enough for him to understand. Now he heard the same thing in her tone. He had wanted to question it but desire had fogged his reasoning.

"I have a notion that you have a low regard for me," he said, stopping in front of her.

Lady Natalie raised her eyes to his but she only regarded him for a moment before turning and attempting to mount the horse herself. She failed. The horse was a Boulonnaise stallion, and she was a slight woman. She could never mount it without help.

"Do you need help?" he asked.

"No," came her curt reply. He didn't know why she was angry with him.

Jasper watched her struggle for a while before he decided to intervene. "You need my help," he said, taking hold of her shoulders. She stilled and allowed him to turn her. *Heavens, she is lovely!* His hands circled her small waist and he lifted her onto the saddle. "There."

Lady Natalie bit her lip again, and he held a groan. She drew his gaze to her mouth every time she did that. Was she asking for another kiss? Taking a breath, he loosened the horse's tether, and he climbed up behind her, taking the reins. She stiffened slightly, and he chuckled.

"You have nothing to fear, My Lady."

"You are the Masked Rogue."

Was that why she was angry with him? *No, it cannot be. She didn't know this last night.* "I thought you had no care for your reputation."

"I did not with a duke. You are a different issue entirely."

He steered them onto the road that led out of the park. "But I *am* a duke."

Lady Natalie sighed and shook her head, seemingly disinclined to continue the conversation. He rode steadily but the feel of her posterior very close to his groin, despite his cloak, made his heart pound and his blood rush. This forced him to ride faster.

"Where is your house?" he asked as they exited the park.

"Berkeley Square." She sounded breathless, and it both delighted and hardened him.

Every minute of the ride was a challenge, and Jasper fought the relief he felt when they neared her home. A part of him wanted the sweet torment to continue. "Show me the house."

Lady Natalie directed him and he guided the horse into the alley where the side entrance was located. He dismounted and helped her down, but he kept his hands at her waist, the temptation to pull her into his arms and ravish her mouth, growing.

Their gazes held, and she seemed to lean into him. "Your Grace," she whispered, and he shook his head.

"Jasper. Call me, Jasper, please."

"I should go, Jasper." She made to remove his cloak, but he was still unable to let her go.

"Forgive me," he murmured, before pulling her to him and claiming the lips that had consumed his thoughts since waking. He swallowed her gasp, and it turned into a sigh that seared him with need. Jasper drew her ever closer, his hand descending to cup her posterior, pressing his aching pelvis into her.

"I should not kiss you, Jasper," she murmured as his mouth moved to her delicate neck. He wanted to kiss every inch of her if she would allow him.

"No, you should not," he agreed, but he did not stop. He claimed her mouth again, exploring every inch with passionate determination. Every little moan excited him, and his fingers curled, gathering her skirts.

I have to stop, he told himself, yet all he wanted was to place her back on his horse and ride away with her. She was not the sort of woman he should do this to, but he could not help what she did to him. Drawing every bit of willpower he could, he stopped kissing her and pulled away.

Bloody hell! Her lips were swollen, and her eyelids were heavy. She was the very image of seduction, even though she was fully clothed and shrouded by his cloak. Lady Natalie started toward the door, but she paused and reached for the pin that kept his cloak in place.

Jasper inhaled sharply as he watched her pull the heavy garment away to reveal a luscious body that her wet dress still clung to. When she breathed, her neckline pressed tightly against her soft bosom, and he was sure that if he touched her, he would feel her nipples perking in response to the cold.

As she handed the cloak to him, their eyes held, and he saw her hesitation. She shared his wish to not part at this time. Jasper took the cloak at the same time that his arm snaked around her waist, drawing her back to him. She raised her chin, and he reclaimed her mouth as her eyes fluttered shut. Their passions interwove as his hand grasped her hair, deepening the kiss.

He moved them until her back was against a wall. Hiking up her skirt, he reached underneath and stroked her thighs, and her shivers heightened his fervor, causing every part of him to grow rigid with want.

A distant sound forcefully broke them apart once more, but this time, they remained close together. Her eyes gleamed, and although he could not tell whether she blushed, he knew she did. She also looked surprised. Leaning forward, he kissed her delectable lips one final time. When she spoke, her voice was soft—excessively so. "Good night, Jasper."

"Sleep well, My Lady." His voice did not quite sound like his. She moved past him to open the door, and he watched her disappear behind it, passing a hand down his jaw as he hoped to see her again soon. He had to finish what they had begun or thoughts of her would never leave him.

Jasper rode to the townhouse he dedicated to his nightly activities, and looking carefully around to ensure he was not recognized or followed, he moved into the alley where he secured his stallion before unlocking the door on the side of the house and entering.

Taking the stairs, he went to his bedchamber and removed his damp clothes before they gave him a cold. Then he left the house again, unmasked this time, and rode for an hour to Amsthorne Manor. Jasper made a promise to his aunt some time ago that he would always return to the manor and spend the night there if he was in town.

She disliked being alone, and she also worried about him, especially after the first discussion they had about the family's curse two years ago. Jasper arrived and took the horse to the stables and made sure it was comfortably in its stall, then he made his way into the manor.

He found his valet, Smith, in his chambers, and the first thing he did was hand him his mask. The leather strap had snapped when Natalie—he could not think of her formally any longer—removed it.

"Have another one made," he instructed. Smith was the only person who knew he was the Masked Rogue, and he was fortunate to have his confidence.

Jasper sat in a chair, thinking of Natalie. He had to see her again, and there was no question in his mind.

Chapter Seven

A woman was saved by the Masked Rogue last night at Hyde Park. We have good cause to believe that she is one of his mistresses. How quaint! Is this a clue about the existence of a heart?

Jasper sat at the breakfast table and glanced at the papers that had been set down for him. One was The Times, and the other was The Londoner. He picked up the latter with a broad grin. It was the paper he read every morning, for he enjoyed watching England speculate and attempt to unmask him.

One of the scoundrels told The Londoner everything. Yes, they reported themselves, but who would not when the Masked Rogue is involved? There was no one at Hyde Park at the hour to tell us what occurred after the Rogue chased the brigands away with a pistol, but we will find that woman, and she will lead us to our dear hero.

. . .

JASPER LAUGHED. YESTERDAY'S REPORT CALLED HIM A SCOUNDREL, and now he was a hero. He wondered what he would be tomorrow. They will never find Natalie. He will make sure of it. Whoever wrote for The Londoner appeared to be obsessed with the Masked Rogue, and he found it most amusing. He set the paper down and filled a cup with coffee.

He raised his gaze when his aunt walked into the room, then he stopped what he was doing and rose, going to greet her. She turned her cheek away when he attempted to kiss it.

"Is something the matter?" he asked with a chuckle. She was trying to be angry with him.

Phoebe sat in the chair across from him at the round table, and he picked up a plate, filling it with everything he knew she would like. Then Jasper circled the table and set it down in front of her. She still did not respond, but her countenance shifted very slightly.

He returned to his seat and took a sip of coffee, studying her. After a while, he leaned back in his seat. "You are angry with me, Aunt Phoebe," he said.

"Yes, I am," she replied, piercing a sausage with her fork.

"Will you tell me what it is I did?" He started reaching for the paper but thought the better of it. Her mood might worsen if she saw him reading instead of listening to her. Jasper had an inkling of why she was like this.

"You did not walk with Miss Gilmore yesterday."

I knew it! "I never promised I would come."

"But you should have," Phoebe countered petulantly.

"Is that the only thing?" Jasper raised one eyebrow.

"No," his aunt straightened. "That was merely the introduction. You are not being entirely honest with me, Jasper. You leave the manor in the evenings and stay out for long hours. Your absence has worsened in the last several weeks, and you did not have dinner here yesterday."

He closed his eyes and sighed. "I had business in town."

"With your mistress?" she inquired, tilting her head.

"Does it matter with whom?"

"Yes, it does. You owe your title a debt, and I encourage you to pay it. Miss Gil—"

"I will pay my debt when the time is right, Auntie." He rose and walked over to her, placing a hand on her shoulder. "We should not spoil a good morning with such conversations."

"When is a better time to discuss?" She looked up at him with worried eyes.

"Certainly not today, Auntie." He was in a good mood today, and he did not want anything to ruin it.

Phoebe took his hand and squeezed. "Whatever is troubling you, Jasper, you know you can tell me."

She had never—and likely never would—believe what truly troubled him. He kissed the back of her hand. "Of course." He returned to his seat and resumed his reading.

"Good heavens, Jasper!" Phoebe gasped a moment later. He looked up at her with a frown. "When will you stop reading that nonsense?"

"This?" He raised the gossip sheet.

"Society has infected you with its obsession. Honestly, I do not see the reason to follow one man and make life difficult for him."

"And how do you know life is difficult for the Rogue?"

"He must be weary of reading about himself every day."

Jasper chuckled. "Perhaps."

"I have to admire his insolence and wit," she continued. "For six years, no one has been able to discover anything about him."

And they never shall, he added quietly. "And you accuse me of being infected by society," he teased. His aunt was fond of the Masked Rogue, but she would never admit it.

He spent the remainder of the meal listening to her compliment and condemn the Rogue all at once, saying she was only making observations whenever he pointed out her admiration. When breakfast was over, he rose to leave.

"I am having tea this afternoon with new acquaintances. Would you like to join us?"

Jasper shook his head. "You know I rarely join you for tea."

"Would you not want to be introduced to the young ladies? If you are disinterested in courting Miss Gilmore, then perhaps these might capture your attention. They are Miss Gilmore's acquaintances."

Excellent reasons I should not be introduced to them. "I have quite the day ahead of me, Auntie. Another time, perhaps." Phoebe grumbled and waved for him to leave. "I shall compensate you for this," he said on his way out.

"I shall collect, then," she replied, and he laughed. She was such a dear, and he would have loved to spend more time with her this morning, but he had to meet with his solicitor.

Time was against him, and he must ensure his Will was in order.

NATALIE JABBED A NEEDLE INTO THE VELVET SHE WAS HEMMING with lace and mumbled to herself. She had managed to sleep upon her return due to weariness, but her waking thoughts were not quiet.

She was grateful to Jasper for rescuing her, and her discomposure, the kiss, and...everything else, had caused her to forget to thank him, but she found it utterly unbelievable that he was the Masked Rogue of London.

The secret she sought had found her the night before, and all she had to do was tell Hannah he was the Rogue, and her eleventh wish would be fulfilled. Yet, Natalie could not bring herself to do so.

No matter what she thought of him, he had saved her, and one act of kindness deserved another. Hannah's voice pierced her concentration as she walked into the sitting room on the second floor, and Natalie looked up.

Her cousin shook what looked like a copy of The Londoner. "Someone gave them something more exciting that happened last night and they did not publish what I wrote about the Masked Rogue's new wager with a Baron.

Natalie's eyes widened. "What happened?" she asked despite almost certainly knowing. She was hoping no one had recognized her.

Hannah gave her the sheet and she read quickly, secretly heaving a sigh of relief when she found nothing to identify her. "I must find the woman he rescued. The Londoner would have to publish that story and pay me for it."

Natalie forced herself to smile in encouragement. "Yes, you must."

"She is all everyone is talking about. Some claim she is his mistress, and others are conjecturing she is a lady of the ton."

Natalie's stomach turned, and she set the dress down and stood, suddenly restless and pretending to fetch a fabric. "Why would they think she is a lady when they never saw her?"

"I cannot say," Hannah sat in a chair, and wisps of her dark hair fell over her eyes, forcing her to blow them away. "I wonder if the lady saw his face."

"He would not allow anyone to see his face." Jasper's secret weighed heavily on her, and she was afraid a simple expression could reveal the truth to Hannah.

"What if she did?" Hannah insisted.

"Then someone knows his face, and history has been made."

Her cousin shot to her feet. "I have to find this woman. She is the key, Natalie! Think of the reward when we unmask him!" She flew out of the room before Natalie could say anything.

She sighed and flopped back onto the sofa. Knowing was difficult, and this was only the first day. Hannah poked her head back into the room, her eyes wide.

"Do you think he loves her?"

"Heavens, no!" Natalie blurted, and her cousin blinked.

"Quite a passionate response."

"I am horrified on the woman's behalf," she said, recovering quickly. "Who would want such a man's love, Hannah?"

"Indeed!" Her cousin left again, while she sank into the sofa, remembering their kiss.

Jasper had held her tenderly and sweetly, and her body had responded in a way that she never imagined. He might be the first man to kiss her, but she was not without knowledge of what happened between a man and a woman. She had read books and heard women talk. Some talked freely in front of her now that she was a spinster.

"Natalie!" Hannah called, and she sat up. Her cousin ran into the room, her face pink. "Lady Phoebe's invitation just arrived!" She threw a note on Natalie's lap.

Endeavoring to be calm, she read the invitation, almost dropping it when she saw that Lady Phoebe was requesting their presence this afternoon. That was sooner than she anticipated. Too soon.

Her nerves fluttered at the prospect of seeing Jasper. She knew she would see him again, but not so soon. "It is almost time," Natalie declared. "We should prepare."

They dressed, and within an hour, they were in a carriage and riding to Amsthorne Manor. Hannah talked throughout to contain her excitement, while Natalie tried to breathe.

When they arrived, Lady Phoebe received them cheerfully in the drawing room. "I wanted to introduce you to my nephew, the Duke of Amsthorne," she said as they sat, "but he is a very busy man. Sadly, I shan't be making any introductions today."

"Another time, My Lady," Hannah said, and Natalie wondered if she would be pleased to be introduced to Jasper if she knew he was the reason they were in dire financial difficulty. Her cousin had been thirteen years old when it happened, and neither Natalie nor George felt the need to tell her everything as she grew older. Natalie might have to tell her at some point, however.

"I am sure he will join us next time," Lady Phoebe said, sounding certain her nephew would be there.

Natalie found herself equal parts relieved and disappointed. The relief she understood clearly but the disappointment perplexed her. She had been anxious to see him, but it didn't explain why she would feel, thusly.

Tea was very pleasant, and Natalie found Lady Phoebe to be more agreeable than she thought. They shared several opinions, and she was surprised when Lady Phoebe said, "I cannot understand why a lady cannot have a trade."

Hannah's eyes gleamed. "It strikes me with anguish that she cannot write and have her name known and associated with her craft."

"Yes, my dear. Perhaps it will change someday, but before then, we may do as we please in secret."

Natalie laughed at that, thinking of the dresses and bonnets she made in secret. She could not tell Lady Phoebe about them even though they were speaking freely. She was not confident enough to do so.

"Will you be attending Lady Barton's ball next week?"

"Yes, My Lady," Natalie replied.

"It is going to be a grand event," Lady Phoebe shrugged as though she was not pleased with the scale of the ball, "and many will leave their country homes to attend, but I am looking forward to seeing you there."

Natalie smiled. "So are we, My Lady."

Three hours later, they returned home. Natalie and Hannah were chatting animatedly as they entered the house, but the sight of the physician in the front hall with the butler stopped them.

Natalie knew why he was there, and her heart sank. "Dr. Rivers, is something wrong?" she asked after the physician had greeted them. They had known the middle-aged man for years, and he had tended to her father in his final days.

"I came to examine Lord Clifford, My Lady."

She glanced at the butler and saw how he was avoiding her gaze. "What happened to him?"

"His Lordship needs ample rest to recover," Dr. Rivers said, and she knew he was not telling her everything to spare her sensibilities.

"You do not have to be modest with me, Doctor."

"Well," Dr. Rivers looked at the butler, "I was told he fainted. He was awake when I arrived, but my examination found him weak and in want of rest and nutrition."

Natalie swallowed. "I will ensure he rests and eats well. Thank you, Doctor."

"I shall return tomorrow." He bowed. "I bid you a good day, My Lady."

Hannah was already climbing the stairs to find George, and Natalie followed her. She stopped in the doorway of his bedchamber and watched as Hannah went to hug him. Natalie clenched her jaw and schooled her features before walking in.

He looked pale and thin, and when their eyes met, tears stung her throat. She hated seeing him like this, and she could not help feeling it was all her fault. If she had acted differently, he would have inherited the title with a good fortune. He could be living like a lord, attending society events, spending his evenings at gentlemen's clubs... Natalie mentally shook herself.

"I told Dr. Rivers not to say anything to you," George said when Hannah asked him how he was.

"We have the right to know about your condition, George," Natalie said calmly, sitting beside him on the bed and taking his hand. "How can we look after you if we do not know?"

"I shall be well," he reassured them.

"Did Dr. Rivers leave instructions for your care?" Natalie asked.

"Only rest and nutrition."

"You have not been eating well, George," Hannah pointed out, "and you drink more than we do."

"Naturally," George chuckled, but neither Natalie nor his sister joined him. Sighing, he said, "I will eat more."

"Do you promise?" Hannah implored.

"Yes," he replied, while guilt continued to scratch Natalie's insides. There had to be a better way for their family's finances to recover without George working himself to an early grave. She had to seek that way.

Chapter Eight

As we end the chapter of Lord Mansfield, we open another, which should remind us of how ruthless our Masked Rogue is. Baron Peckhart lost a wager, and although it was not a significant sum, word is that he was shamed at the club. Is this how we will allow an unknown man to disgrace the aristocracy?

"You are relentless, Hannah," Natalie sighed.

They were standing near the refreshment table in Lady Barton's filled ballroom a week later, and Hannah, who saw an opportunity to investigate instead of seeking a suitor, was scribbling on a small piece of parchment with a pencil.

"I must know, Natalie. The reward The Londoner is offering will help us. I heard it is a pretty fortune."

Natalie shook her head and allowed her eyes to move across the room. They had seen and exchanged greetings with Lady Phoebe earlier, but she was drawn away by the hostess. Like Natalie, Jasper's aunt was a spinster, but society appeared to have forgiven her and forgotten about it.

It was unfair, but Natalie had to bear it. Even though she stood with Hannah by the refreshment table, she felt unwanted and unwelcome.

"Who do you think the lady is?" her cousin asked. "Do you think she is here?"

Natalie's eyebrows drew together. "You are asking me?"

"Not you, but..." She trailed off at the sight of the handsome gentleman approaching them. Her cousin's cheeks turned a vibrant shade of pink, and she appeared to know the man.

When Natalie looked from Hannah to the gentleman, her cousin introduced them. "Lord Wessberg, this is my cousin, Lady Natalie Reeves." She grinned at her. "Natalie, Viscount Wessberg. He helped me answer some questions at the puppet player's stall that earned me the ballerina."

"Oh." Natalie smiled at it. "It is a pleasure to make your acquaintance, My Lord."

"Likewise." He placed a kiss on her knuckles.

Wessberg asked Hannah to dance, and Natalie was glad she had been able to make them new dresses in time for the ball. A viscount had taken interest in her cousin, and with luck, she would make a match before next season. It was all Natalie and George could hope for.

As she stood alone, she saw several ladies in the distance look and point in her direction. Natalie picked up a glass of punch and tried to look occupied with it as pathetic as that seemed. She dared to glance up, and she saw more eyes turning in her direction, causing her to press her lips together. She had told herself many times that society's rejection no longer affected her, but all she had to do was attend a ball to be reminded of everything.

Picking up a small cake, she took a bite, then winced at its dryness, setting it down and sipping some punch. Still feeling awkward and desperate, she contemplated leaving the ballroom and venturing into the garden. There were not many people there, and she could find the escape she needed.

"Lady Natalie."

Her breath caught, and she turned around slowly, the air leaving her lungs completely at the sight of Jasper. Natalie was, once more, struck by how handsome he was. She curtsied politely. "Your Grace."

He took her gloved hand and kissed it, then his other hand joined, placing something between her fingers. "I would have asked you to dance but..." He glanced behind him at the crush of people in the ballroom. There was space to dance, but getting to the floor was a journey by itself. "Why are you here by yourself?" he asked.

"I like being by myself," she lied. Natalie did not mind solitude, but not at a ball.

Smiling, he looked down at her hand, silently gesturing for her to examine what he had placed there. She looked down to find a small piece of paper. "I hope to see you soon," Jasper said, walking past her to the glass doors that led out to the garden.

Natalie unfolded the paper and read, her heart beating faster:

Meet me in the garden.

Chapter Nine

A house in Whitechapel is said to be the Rogue's residence. He cannot be a gentleman if that is where his home is. More proof is required, and we believe we are closer than ever. The woman he rescued is a lady; one with dark hair and green eyes, too. London appears to be in abundance of dark-haired ladies. Where to look?

Reading the note, Natalie was transported back to a memory from nine years ago. Jasper had asked her to meet him in the library, that he had something to show her. Giddy and supposedly in love, she snuck out of the ballroom to meet him.

They were introduced that night, but Natalie had known and admired him longer. Believing she had found the man who would become her husband, she met him alone, and he charmed her.

Now, closing her eyes and breathing, she straightened her shoulders. She would meet him in the garden, but the time for mistakes had long passed. Jasper could not charm her now or corrupt her reputation. An inexplicable desire existed between them but that was all it was. Simple desire.

Placing the note in her reticule, she looked around the ballroom once, then turned and stepped out into the terrace. She walked to the balustrade and stood by it, her eyes sweeping the garden in search of him. Several guests milled about the terrace but they hardly took any notice of her.

She caught movement on her right and turned, seeing Jasper beneath a topiary arch. Then he turned and walked away. She followed him, descending the short steps and taking a cobbled path. He disappeared, but Natalie continued walking until she felt his hand circle her wrist, and he drew her behind a tall hedge.

"Natalie," he murmured, and her breath quickened.

"I did not give you leave to use my Christian name."

Jasper tilted his head. "I cannot continue to address you formally after everything that happened between us," he whispered. "You know my deepest secret."

"Is this why you called me here?" she asked.

"Yes, and to ask for another kiss." He gave her a wicked smile.

"You cannot ask for a kiss, Jasper. You will not have one." Her body contradicted her words by warming and yearning.

"We shall see." He folded his arms across his broad chest. "I trust you did not tell anyone what you saw last night."

Natalie bristled. "Why would I?"

"Surely, you do not expect me to be secure in the knowledge that you will keep what you witnessed to yourself without inquiring and ensuring you do," he said. "I am society's greatest obsession." He sounded proud of himself just then.

"You have that wrong. The Rogue is society's obsession, not you," Natalie challenged.

He chuckled. "That is a good point, but we are the same person. You appear to have separated us in your mind."

She had to separate them because they were different to her. *Is he truly?* she mused, wondering what story he was hiding behind the mask. He could not have created the Masked Rogue without a reason.

Something moved deep in his blue eyes but he blinked, and it disappeared before she could capture and understand it. "What is your price?" he asked abruptly.

"I beg your pardon?" Natalie thought that she heard him wrong.

"The price of your silence," he elaborated, and she felt insulted that he thought he could throw money at her and have her keep his secret. Did he know about her family's troubles? Most of society did. It was no secret that she and Hannah had no dowry. It was another thing that propelled her spinsterhood.

She thought of Oliver, and how he had demanded his silence be bought. *Why does this not surprise me?* Jasper and Oliver were friends, and they were likely to think alike, which wounded her pride even more.

Natalie opened her mouth to tell him what she thought of his behavior but paused when a notion formed in her mind. She had a list to complete, and most of the activities could not be accomplished without help. Who better to help her enter a gentleman's club or fence than the Masked Rogue of London?

"The price of my silence is heavy, Jasper," she said. "Are you willing to pay it?"

"Whatever it is."

"I have a list…" she began, her doubt rising, but she pushed it down. "Things I want to accomplish. I cannot do some of them by myself."

"You need my help," he stated.

"I need *his* help," she corrected.

He grinned. "Done."

Natalie blinked. "You have not heard what I want."

"I do not believe in impossibilities. I am sure they are daring activities, judging by your trip to my home to kiss me, and swimming in the Serpentine."

A thrill of excitement and anticipation rushed through Natalie at her victory. "In fact, I have just accomplished one thing tonight." She only just realized it.

"What is that?" He cocked a brow.

"Sneak away with a gentleman at a ball."

Amusement curved his mouth. "Oh? Is that all sneaking away with a gentleman is to you?"

"What more can it be?" She knew the answer, but she wanted to tease him. The gleam in his eyes gave her confidence she struggled to draw out at any other time.

"Let me show you." He took a step toward her, and Natalie's body was set aflame by his closeness. Placing a finger beneath her chin, he whispered, "May I?"

At her nod, he kissed her softly, his arms circling her waist and pressing her into him. His musky scent filled her senses, and passion engulfed the rest of her. Natalie raked her fingers through his raven hair as he moved them further behind the hedge.

His body was hard and warm, such that she did not feel the bite of the air. Their kiss grew in intensity, and his hand squeezed her posterior, melting her core and arousing her in the deepest way she had ever felt. She moaned his name, and it encouraged him.

Kissing a trail down her neck, he pulled down the neckline of her blue velvet dress and kissed the swells of her breasts, gliding his tongue sweetly across her skin. She grasped his shoulders to keep upright. Suddenly she felt his mouth around her nipple, and she bit her lip to contain a cry of delight. She did not know how he freed her from her dress, and she did not care. All that mattered at that instant was how he suckled her, and the fiery ripples of pleasure that ran through her body.

Jasper moved to lavish the same attention to her other breast while he hiked her skirts up, slipping his hand underneath and stroking her thighs, and tantalizing her by not touching her where she ached the most.

Laughter in the distance pulled them apart, and Natalie realized with wide eyes that this was not the place for this. There was no one in sight, but she could not continue this no matter how she wanted to. She quickly pulled her dress up, discovering that some of the buttons at the back had been unfastened.

Jasper helped her fasten them, his hands heating her all over again as they brushed her skin. "What is your next wish?" he whispered in her ear.

"Gamble in a gentleman's club," she replied. He turned her around, and his surprise was visible.

"We shall do it. I will inform you of the time soon." He leaned forward and kissed her cheek, and she almost melted in his arms again.

To keep herself from doing that, she turned and gathered her skirt, hurrying away from him. Thankfully, there was no one around the hedges when she left, and she made her way back to the ballroom.

Hannah found her. "Where were you? I have been looking all over the ballroom."

"I was on the terrace seeking...fresh air," she replied, just as she saw Jasper walk into the ballroom. Their eyes met and held, and Natalie saw the promise of adventure in their depths.

Chapter Ten

Before we speak of the usual subject, we would like to bring to everyone's attention that the reclusive Duke of Amsthorne danced with Lady Natalie Reeves at Lady Barton's ball. Could an unexpected courtship be on the horizon? The Masked Rogue was not seen at all last night, and we would conjecture he was at the ball, too.

The following afternoon, Natalie gathered the dress she finished sewing that morning and left the house. Hannah was out riding with Wessberg, which was splendid, while Natalie found herself with ample time.

She rode to Mary's shop, and she was fortunate to find her alone. She gave her the dress, and Mary paid her for it. "I would never have become popular without you, Natalie."

"We help each other, Mary. I am fortunate that you can help me sell my dresses." Mary sewed beautifully but Natalie's dresses were better, and that helped her gain the *ton's* patronage.

They were the same age, and Natalie sometimes found herself envious of Mary's uncomplicated life. She could trade and find independence through it, but Natalie could not. Society tied her worth to a man, and she was unwanted.

Alexandra appeared suddenly, and when she saw Natalie, her expression darkened. Mary rose to attend to her. "I see you are friends with the modiste," she giggled beneath a hand. "Why does that not surprise me."

"What do you hope to accomplish by saying that?" Natalie asked.

"Oh, nothing. It is simply unfortunate that you must grasp to get what you want. I heard you had tea with Lady Phoebe." Alexandra smiled viciously. "Are you friends now? Are you perhaps hopeful that your unmarried state would be something to bond you with her?"

"You will watch your words," Natalie warned. "I thought Lady Phoebe was your friend, too."

Alexandra rolled her eyes, and Natalie guessed she was angry. Mary stood to the side. She would not intervene because her business depended on the *ton's* goodwill.

"I will remind you that Lady Phoebe's situation is by choice. She is wanted, you see…" Alexandra trailed off so the implication of her words hung heavy between them. Natalie swallowed the hurt constricting her throat, but Alexandra was relentless. "Or is it the Duke of Amsthorne you are after by befriending her?"

The mention of Jasper and the memory that passed quickly through her warmed her. The blush gave Alexandra the wrong notion, however, and her blue eyes sparked with vitriol.

"My goodness!" she exclaimed. "It *is* him! You want the Duke!" She looked as though she could not believe it. "He would not look at you, much less give you any attention if you were the last woman in the world, Lady Natalie."

Natalie found leverage then. "You are wrong, Miss Gilmore. You see, we danced last night, and I believe The Londoner carried the news." Alexandra's mouth fell open. "You did not see?"

"I left the ball early," she said through clenched teeth.

Natalie looked around the shop, and when her gaze found the gossip sheet, she picked it up and handed it to Alexandra. "Good day, Miss Gilmore."

She did not know where the strength to defend herself came from, but she never wanted to allow herself to be insulted again. Nodding at Mary, she left the shop, feeling better than she had in a long while.

Hannah had still not returned from her ride when Natalie returned home, but she found George in the drawing room. He was seated at a table, shuffling some cards.

He was excellent at cards, unbeatable even, and he was also an artist, who painted his cards himself. Everyone in their family was in possession of great talent. It was just unfortunate that fate tried them. The liquor in a glass beside him told her that something was bothering him more than usual.

"May I join you?" she asked from the doorway.

"Of course, Natalie."

She sat on his right and touched his arm. "You can talk to me. You know that, do you not?"

He gave her a warm smile. "And have you worry excessively?"

"I am stronger than I look, George."

He set the cards down and took both of her hands. "Your father said the same thing when he asked me to look after you. I have no doubt in your strength, but I have no wish to burden you."

"You will not burden me, George," she reassured him. "You will instead share what troubles you. I am sure you will feel better if you do."

George sighed. "If you insist. Oliver made numerous investments abroad with funds from our coal mining business. The factory is short of funds, and we hardly gain anything from our share." Anger simmered in her chest, and she clenched her teeth. "We might have to find a small cottage in the country and leave town."

Natalie blinked furiously. Oliver had taken everything from them, and he was still taking more. When will he stop? When they were completely penurious and begging on the streets? "Viscount Wessberg might be courting Hannah," she said to brighten the grim atmosphere.

"A courtship is not an offer," George sighed.

"But we can hope. For Hannah's sake, we should wait until we know the Viscount's true intentions."

"You are right, as always." George managed a smile. "I do feel better after telling you, and your advice is invaluable."

"I am glad I could help. Perhaps we can lessen the household further. I think one maid and a footman are enough. I can manage the house without the housekeeper."

"Quite so," he agreed. "I will give it some thought."

Natalie dearly hoped that Wessberg would marry Hannah. Once she secured a match, Natalie could leave London with George. Life in the country would be fairer and better for her. Her cousin would be healthier, too.

He released her hands and stood, looking down dolefully at her. He looked gaunt and pale, and her heart ached.

"I will go to the club now," he said. She knew he was seeking a distraction from their troubles.

Fresh anger boiled in her blood. Natalie still blamed Jasper but perhaps she should focus her rage on Oliver, too. After all, he was the one who extorted them. One or both of these men had to pay.

Chapter Eleven

The Masked Rogue was not allowed in establishments as fine as White's and Brooks, but there are clubs on the fringes that welcome him. We must never allow such a man to truly be a part of us. But what if he is a gentleman? This certainly would change everything.

Jasper was spending his afternoon at White's, and all he could think of was his arrangement with Natalie. He wanted to know why she had that list, but he was also excited to help her. He would see her as often as he wished and collect his kisses. He could not seem to have enough.

His idle gaze landed on the Earl of Clifford shuffling some cards at the far end of the room, and at that instant, he recalled the debts the man had. Natalie was his cousin, and she was affected by it.

He frowned. Was that why she had the list? To help her survive their misfortune?

Society was of the opinion that the present Earl had squandered the fortunes and sold the once very successful coal business to Oliver, but

Jasper was not one to believe words carried about. The late earl made mistakes that placed the coal factory in difficulty, and Oliver purchased it from him because he saw a good opportunity.

Jasper had never cared before, but because of Natalie, he was incredibly curious now. He watched Clifford help himself to a generous amount of liquor from the decanter on his table. Deciding to join him, Jasper rose and picked up his brandy, walking over to him.

"May I?" He pointed to the empty seat opposite Clifford.

Clifford looked surprised, but nodded, carrying on with shuffling his cards. After a moment, he paused and pushed the decanter toward Jasper. "You may drink with me if you like, Your Grace."

Indulging him, Jasper splashed a little more brandy into his glass and took a sip, his gaze settling on the cards. It was a deck he had never seen before. Clifford saw him looking and said, "I paint them myself." He gave Jasper a suit to examine.

The skill was impressive, and the art was medieval in style. "These are excellent cards, Clifford. Do you mind selling them to me?"

Clifford shook his head. "I did not paint them to sell, Your Grace."

"Will you play me for them, then?" Jasper offered, knowing quite well that Clifford did not gamble. For a man in dire want of funds, he never indulged. It took great character and strength, and Jasper admired him.

Clifford considered his offer for a while before he nodded. "I suppose I should defend my cards."

"Indeed."

He collected the remaining cards from Jasper and began to shuffle them again. "Piquet?"

"Yes."

Jasper called a footman to bring them a sheet and a pencil to keep their scores.

The first round began, and what Jasper thought would be a quick and easy match turned out to be a challenging one. Soon, gentlemen gathered around them to watch, and they made wagers between themselves.

Jasper scarcely gambled, but the Masked Rogue did, and he was undefeated. It would seem he had found a worthy match in Clifford today, and at the end of the last round, Clifford was declared the victor.

Of course, most of the gentlemen lost their wagers because they bet against the Earl. Jasper laughed as the men grumbled in disbelief. "It has been long since I was last defeated, Clifford." Defeat felt unfamiliar but he perceived it as a challenge.

"Then you have never played against the Masked Rogue," Clifford chuckled. He looked better than he did before their game, but Jasper noticed how thin he was.

"There are some risks I cannot take," he replied evenly. "The Masked Rogue will take everything from me."

"Indeed," one gentleman said. "Look at poor Lord Mansfield."

"And now Baron Peckhart," another said.

"I have no wish to see my name in The Londoner again." Jasper returned his attention to the cards. "I will want those, Clifford."

"Then you must win them fairly from me," the Earl declared.

"Yes, we should have another round," someone suggested. "I will happily bet on Clifford now."

Jasper was tempted to put money in the wager to help him if he won, but he had an inkling that Clifford would not appreciate it. This feeling of generosity confused him, and he did not know where it was coming from.

They began another game, and Clifford gained several points against Jasper in the first round. The gentlemen with wagers on him began to rejoice.

"My Lord," someone said to Clifford, "you should play against the Masked Rogue."

"I agree," another shouted in jest. "We should choose Lord Clifford as our champion against the Rogue. He is cleaving our fortunes. We must defend ourselves!"

Jasper laughed at their spirit. He would happily play at this little war they were waging, but he would not accept Clifford as their champion. He was beginning to see that what had been said about him was untrue. He did not look like a man who would squander a fortune. He did not gamble, and his name had never been mentioned in stories involving deceit and treachery—besides in the rumors.

On seeing that he was losing, Jasper played every trick that would favor him, and he still lost. The room erupted in cheer, and the gentlemen declared Clifford the champion of the aristocracy against the Masked Rogue of London.

"Those cards are precious to you, are they not?" Jasper asked, rising.

"They are," Clifford replied with what looked like an earnest smile.

"We will play again, Clifford. I wish to have them."

"And I shall defend them again, Your Grace."

Jasper inclined his head before leaving. If he had lost to any other man, he would have felt the desire to continue playing until he won his honor, but something about Clifford softened him, and he suspected it was Natalie.

***

"Your name was in The Londoner, but I am pleased," Phoebe said as they ate dinner.

"Why are you pleased?"

"You made the acquaintance of Lady Natalie. She is the one I wanted to introduce you to last week."

Jasper lowered the bite of roast beef he was guiding to his mouth. "You had tea with Lady Natalie?"

"Yes." His aunt grinned. "You were much too occupied to join us," she reminded him.

He almost told her that he would have joined them if he had known it was Natalie. He kept it to himself, however. Jasper did not want to give her hope that he would marry.

"You do not have to court Miss Gilmore. Lady Natalie is good enough to become the Duchess of Amsthorne."

Jasper's fork stopped halfway to his mouth again. "Dancing with her is not akin to courting her."

"But you *can* court her," his aunt emphasized with a smirk.

"We should speak of something else," he suggested.

"Very well," she sighed. "I have finished writing all the invitations to your name day ball. Once you review them, I will have them delivered."

He was hosting a grand ball for his thirty-fifth birthday to bid society farewell. It would be one of the grandest events London had ever seen. As he thought about it, something twisted in his heart, and his fingers tightened around his fork.

Phoebe made him feel worse when she said, "Oh, it feels so long ago when you were my five-year-old boy, and I read you stories and sang you to sleep." She sighed, and he closed his eyes.

Please, do not do this to me, Auntie.

Clearing his throat, he responded. "Perhaps we should travel back in time to relive the memories."

"I wish we could." She placed a hand on his arm. "Would that not be wonderful?"

"Quite so." His voice was thick, and he set down his fork, quite unable to breathe.

"I wish your parents were here to see the man you have grown into," Phoebe continued, wringing his heart without any clue of his suffering. It did not take long for her to acknowledge his changed demeanor, and she asked, "Are you well?"

Jasper shot to his feet and stalked out of the room, tugging at his neckcloth and opening his mouth to take in as much air as he could. His heart raced in terror, and the looming threat moved ever closer. It was already November, and his birthday was in December.

He marched to his study and poured some liquor into a tumbler, downing it in one gulp. It burned a trail down his throat, and he relished the pain. Then he opened a drawer and retrieved the black mask inside, tucking it into his coat, before striding out and demanding his cloak and gloves.

Jasper chose a different gaming hell tonight, one in the East End, and he rode hard and fast. He wanted to outrun the shadow chasing him, but he knew nothing he did would keep death from coming for him.

Chapter Twelve

Someone must have done something sinister in this country, and the Masked Rogue of London is our punishment. East End was graced by his presence last night. He broke into a gentleman's warehouse and encouraged thieves to steal ale. The streets might have been washed clean by the contents of the broken barrels but the stain on London will be eternal. What is happening to our dear town, ladies and gentlemen?

Natalie was in her bedchamber after breakfast, cutting the ivory satin she had purchased from Mary, still unsure what to do with it when Hannah barged into the room.

As always, her face was pink, and her eyes were bright with the news she had brought. "I received word early this morning about The Rogue, and The Londoner published it!"

She handed Natalie the sheet. But Natalie frowned as she read about the rampage Jasper led in East End. What disturbed her was why he would make men pillage another man's property.

"The Rogue was wild last night!" Hannah bounced on the balls of her feet.

"Why would he do this?" Natalie asked, more to herself, but her cousin responded.

"That is what I am going to find next. I think he is mad."

"What gave you that thought?" Natalie asked, once more, thinking about the reason why Jasper created the Rogue.

"You did not finish reading, but never mind. I will tell you." Hannah sat beside her on the bed. "He not only gambled and led a conquest last night, but he also rejected every woman that neared him. He has never done that before. He is mad with love."

Natalie's insides fluttered. His rejecting women did not mean anything. He could simply have not been in the mood for passion.

"You look as though you do not believe me, Natalie."

"I do not know what to believe," Natalie feigned surprise. "Everything about the Masked Rogue is speculation. No one truly knows anything."

"Yes, but he was seen without a woman—"

"Is that unnatural?" Natalie laughed.

"For the Rogue, yes, it very much is. The man known as the rake of rakes…"

The mention of rake moved Natalie's thoughts to her list. She was yet to kiss a rake, and the Masked Rogue was one. She had kissed Jasper, a supposedly perfect gentleman. She could kiss the Rogue to complete that wish, even though they were the same man. After all, there was no rule regarding the order or requirement to complete the list. Though she *had* kissed him the night when he returned her to her home, it wasn't the same as he had removed his mask then.

"Natalie?"

She blinked and turned to look at Hannah. "Yes?"

"You are awfully distracted today. Is something the matter?"

Natalie shook her head. "No, nothing is wrong. What were you saying?"

"I was wondering if it is the woman he rescued at the park – if she is the one he loves."

She shrugged. "You will have to search and discover, Hannah."

"Yes! He risked exposing himself by fighting the scoundrels that night. He would never have done that if he did not have a heart. A heart that could love."

"He does not have a heart," Natalie mumbled to herself, thinking he truly did not have a heart if he could ruin her reputation and forget about it. She was sure now that he had no recollection of the event.

As Hannah continued talking about the Rogue, more questions came to Natalie's mind. What motivated the Rogue? What made him different from the Duke within? But more importantly, what birthed the Masked Rogue?

She felt an overwhelming curiosity take control of her. She wanted to know everything she could about both Jasper and the Rogue.

At three that afternoon, Viscount Wessberg called upon them and invited Hannah for a walk at the park. Naturally, the invitation was extended to Natalie, and she went to Hyde Park with them.

She walked slowly behind Hannah and Wessberg, studying them and looking for anything that would assure her of his intentions. Hannah was not desperate to make a match, but Natalie was for her. George had told her that the Viscount was a good man. If Hannah married him, she would be cared for and protected.

"Lady Natalie!" someone called, and when she turned around, she saw Lady Phoebe leaving a group of ladies and walking toward her.

"My Lady," Natalie greeted with a polite curtsy.

"How glad I am to see you this afternoon." Lady Phoebe looped their arms, and they continued following Hannah. "You did not tell me you are acquainted with my nephew."

"I made his acquaintance a week ago when I encountered him with Miss Gilmore," Natalie explained.

"You were too modest to tell me, were you not?" Lady Phoebe chuckled. "It is quite well. I am happy you met. Your waltz is all everyone is talking about. Did you read The Londoner?"

"Yes, I did, My Lady." Someone else had written that piece, because Hannah wrote only about the Rogue. "What was His Grace's reaction?" Natalie added, curious.

Lady Phoebe raised a mischievous brow. "He reads The Londoner every day, you know. He is not displeased by the news if that is your question."

Natalie wondered if Jasper's aunt knew he was the Masked Rogue, and she was thinking of subtly inquiring when Lady Phoebe continued talking.

"I think we should sit here and allow them to continue," she suggested, pointing at Hannah and Wessberg. "Of course, we will have our eyes on them." They sat on a bench, and Lady Phoebe regarded Natalie curiously, which made her slightly self-conscious. "I am sure you wonder about my interest, and why I seek a friendship with you, Lady Natalie."

"I do, My Lady," she admitted with a modest smile.

"I see a fellow soul in you, Lady Natalie." Lady Phoebe quickly shook her head when Natalie's brows furrowed very slightly. "Oh, I am, by no means, referring to your situation. Through my interactions with you, I have seen your love for your family. One unfamiliar with you could readily believe Miss Hannah to be your sister."

"She *is* my sister," Natalie said.

"Yes." Lady Phoebe smiled in Hannah's direction. They had stopped beneath a tree, and judging by Hannah's grin and Wessberg's laugh, they were greatly enjoying each other's company. "You value your family as much as I do," Lady Phoebe continued, "and should you and my nephew establish a compatibility, you would be most welcome in our home."

Natalie's cheeks burned, and she looked away. Lady Phoebe was seeing something where there was nothing. What existed between her and Jasper was desire and nothing more. He had no intention to marry her, and she no longer had any hopes of marrying.

"I believe you have everything Amsthorne requires in a duchess, and I will encourage my nephew to—"

"Oh, please do not, My Lady," Natalie protested without thinking.

Lady Phoebe raised an eyebrow. "Why do you not want me to encourage him to court you?"

"Well..." She thought quickly of a response. "He is a very willful man, and I feel he should be allowed to make his choices without influence."

Lady Phoebe tilted her head and watched Natalie for several seconds. "You no longer believe you will find a husband, do you?" she asked, then followed the question with, "Forgive me. I do not mean to unsettle you."

Her questions might be direct but Natalie appreciated both her honesty and her curtness. "On the contrary, My Lady. I am quite pleased with your questions."

Lady Phoebe allowed a soft laugh. "That is a relief, then, and you are correct. My nephew is willful, and one cannot simply make him do anything." A rueful shadow passed over her eyes. "Sometimes, I feel as though I force things upon him. Thus, I must remind myself that I am not his mother, but merely his aunt." The small smile on her lips turned wistful.

Natalie placed a hand on Lady Phoebe's. "I do not think that you are *merely* his aunt." She knew that Jasper's mother died when he was very young—perhaps before Natalie was born. "You are the only mother he knows, and he must be aware of his good fortune." As she said that, she realized that she hoped Jasper was aware of how fortunate he was.

Lady Phoebe's countenance seemed melancholic. Natalie found it unusual because she was most often cheerful.

"Oh, but I am the one grateful to have him, you see," Lady Phoebe said. "I was not always like this." She went on to tell Natalie about her life and how the late Duchess' death had changed her.

Lady Phoebe had met a gentleman, a colonel, during her debut season. Although there had been a considerable difference in their age, they loved each other. His duty to the crown took him away from England, but not without the promise to marry her upon his return.

"Months later, I received a letter from his brother, informing me of his passing," Lady Phoebe finished, and Natalie felt her eyes mist, and her heart break for the woman. She had never been in love, but she had once dreamed of it. She could understand how devastating such a loss could be.

"I am sorry, My Lady," she whispered.

"After his death," Lady Phoebe continued, "I could not find it in myself to accept any other man. Since I am so fond of travel, I left England in the hopes that the adventure would ease my grief. I met many interesting people, drank and gambled excessively," she chuckled and shook her head. "I was essentially wild. I suppose you could refer to me as the female Masked Rogue."

Is Jasper being the Masked Rogue because he was grieving? He could not still be mourning his parents, could he? Or had he lost a woman he loved, too?

"When my sister, the late Duchess of Amsthorne, died, I returned to England." She smiled at Natalie. "I found healing in the little boy's laughter."

Natalie never knew the cause of Lady Phoebe's spinsterhood, and she doubted many people in society did. Her situation was now made to appear glamorous by the *ton*. It was preposterous and unfortunate.

"Oh, pardon my depressing tales, Natalie," Phoebe chuckled sheepishly. "May I call you that?"

"Of course, and you need not apologize for sharing your story with me. I am happy that you allowed me to know you to this extent."

"Then there is no reason for you to continue to address me as Lady Phoebe, is there?" She grinned.

"I suppose not," Natalie giggled, feeling that kinship Phoebe had mentioned earlier. And after learning some of Jasper's tale, she did not feel the overwhelming desire to seek revenge. It was still there but at a low ebb.

Her friendship with Phoebe could shine more light on her path to those secrets she was seeking.

Chapter Thirteen

London's plague was not seen last night. Perhaps he is sitting at a corner in an obscure pub contemplating what he had done. We doubt that is the situation, but a guess is always entertaining. We have learned that the pillaged warehouse belongs to the Marquess of Commerton. How is it that we discover the names of the gentlemen who have fallen prey to the Masked Rogue, yet not the scoundrel himself? What is keeping us from finding him?

Jasper had remained in the manor the night before, not because he did not wish to leave but because he had much to do. He was addressing his will, and that involved poring over everything he possessed, which he learned was more than he had initially thought.

He walked into the breakfast room to see Phoebe seated at the table, sipping tea and perusing The Londoner.

He had not seen her since the dinner he had walked away from, and that was over a day ago. "Good morning, Aunt Phoebe," he greeted, approaching the table.

"I see you have decided to come out of hibernation," she drawled without raising her eyes from the news sheet.

"Yes, Auntie," he replied as he sat across from her, reaching for a cup and filling it with tea from the urn beside him. His head still pounded from the aftermath of drinking excessively the night before. He was aware that he needed to be kinder to his body, but there was nothing else that could stave off the pain in his heart. There was another thing that could help him, but he was not going to depend upon it. "What are the gossips saying about me now?" he asked. "There must be something interesting there if you are unable to put it down."

"There is not a word about you, Jasper."

He gathered that his aunt was still displeased with him, and she had every reason to be. She was a very expressive woman, unafraid to show both her pleasure and displeasure—especially the latter.

"There is always a word about me, Auntie," Jasper chuckled, wincing at the increased throbbing of his head. He waited for Phoebe to ask him what he meant by what he had just said, but she simply turned the single sheet to read the other side, utterly unaware that he had just revealed a hint about him being the Masked Rogue of London.

"Have you always been this conceited, or am I only realizing it now?" Phoebe asked, and he laughed, relieved to hear the jesting tone in her voice.

"You are only discovering it, and a bit too late, if I might add." She set the sheet down, at last, and looked up at him, a tiny smile playing on her lips. "Am I forgiven?" Jasper took her hand and gave it a contrite squeeze. "I did not mean to disrespect or wound you when I left."

"I know you did not, but what displeased me was how abruptly you departed. You know that I will lend you an ear whenever you wish to relieve what grieves you."

He smiled softly at her. "I will come to you, Auntie, but not every time."

"Very well," she sniffed, "You are forgiven, and I shan't dwell on the subject."

"Thank you!" Jasper grinned and raised his teacup to his mouth. He served himself some fruits and cream cheese because his headache would not allow him to eat more than that at this time.

"I wanted to talk to you about Lady Natalie," his aunt said, and his gut tightened, the memories of their encounters rushing back into his mind and hardening his body. Just when he had managed to remove Natalie from his thoughts and rejoiced over his triumph, Phoebe had to remind him of her and cause his battle to begin anew.

"I am not courting her if that is what you wish to inquire about," he said.

"Yes, but I am not blind." Jasper looked up at that, and he saw his aunt's large blue eyes examining him. "I needed only to mention her name, and you shifted in your seat."

His jaw tightened. "What are you saying?"

"That I know you enough to know when you are affected by a woman. You are not indifferent to Lady Natalie, and I want to encourage you to consider proposing to her."

A slice of apple stopped midway to his lips, and he raised an eyebrow. "When I am yet to court her?"

"You do not have to court her," Phoebe laughed. "You already know she would be a good wife for you or any other gentleman who is fortunate enough to have her."

The mention of another gentleman having Natalie made him swallow the bile rising in his throat. His aunt was right, of course. Natalie had the intelligence, poise, and grace to be a duchess. His eyebrows furrowed when the throbbing in his groin became more persistent. She could cure his heartache in the little time he had left, yet he hesitated in his pursuit.

He did not want to leave a young widow, and it would pain him more if that widow was Natalie, but indulging in his desires could wound her just as much. Keeping away from her was not an option he was willing to consider either. Thus, he found himself in quite a conundrum.

"Will you consider it?" Phoebe asked, pulling him from the grasp of his thoughts.

Jasper nodded, but only to placate her. Pleased, she rose and patted his shoulder. "I have to see Cook now to taste samples of the dishes he is preparing for the ball."

After breakfast, Jasper sat in his study and stared at stacks of papers and correspondences on his desk that required his attention. He had to continue going through the particulars of his properties so he would know what to bequeath to whom, but his head pounded as angrily as the devil.

His eyes found the decanter that rested on a table at one end of the room, but he ground his teeth and shook the thought away. He should not indulge in such, especially since liquor was the cause of his troubles this morning.

A knock came at the door then, and he thought he might have found salvation from the task that awaited him. Anything that could draw his attention away was welcome. "Enter!" he answered, wincing at the effort he put forth to be heard.

Smith walked in, then stood to the side to allow a foreman bearing a tray to enter and set it down on a small table by the same chair Natalie sat in the night she had visited him. Jasper allowed a tiny smile, both at the memory and at the sight of the bowl that contained the horrid stew Smith always had made for him when he drank excessively. It was an effective cure, but it tasted like a swamp.

"Where would I be without you, Smith?" he asked once the footman had left, rising and walking over to the soup. "I was just thinking of where to find relief."

"And you did not send for me, Your Grace?" Smith quipped as he moved some papers about the desk to make space for the box he placed atop it.

"I do not particularly enjoy this infernal soup," Jasper returned, wrinkling his nose at the green concoction.

"I am well aware of that, Your Grace," Smith smiled slyly, "and you are most welcome."

Jasper chuckled. It was like this every time Smith brought him the soup. He would say all manner of things about it, but once he ate and felt better, he would thank Smith. "What is that?" he asked, referring to the box on his desk.

"The items you requested, Your Grace."

Jasper set down the soup and strode back to the desk, opening the box immediately. Sitting on a bed of satin was the most magnificent mask he had ever laid eyes upon. Smiling, he picked it up and ran his thumbs along the ivory satin.

"May I ask who the mask is for, Your Grace?" Smith inquired, his curious gaze darting from the mask to Jasper's face and back.

"It is mine, of course," Jasper replied, still staring at the mask before him, positively in awe.

"I beg Your Grace's pardon?" Smith blinked, then stared at him as though he had just declared it the end of the world. "But it is—"

"A woman's?" Jasper supplied, grinning brilliantly as he enjoyed the look of bewilderment on his valet's face. When the man nodded, Jasper added, "I am paying for it; ergo, it is mine."

Smith's puzzlement quickly dissolved into understanding, and he smiled. Jasper went on to instruct him regarding what he planned to do with the mask, then he wrote a note and handed it to him to deliver to Natalie.

Chapter Fourteen

Mayhap the reason we have not uncovered the Masked Rogue's identity is that we relish the ignorance. Who would we speak of in hushed whispers if England's greatest mystery is solved? Yes, Lord Mansfield and Lord Peckhart's gaming misfortunes are diverting, but nothing could save us from ennui if the Rogue is found and the matter closed.

"Natalie."

She raised her head from the lace she was sewing onto a hem to see George in the drawing room doorway. "Yes?"

"May we speak in my study?"

Her stomach flipped despite the fair mood that her cousin appeared to be in. They only spoke in his study when they did not want Hannah to hear them.

"Of course," Natalie answered, setting her task down and gaining her feet.

She followed him to the study, and as soon as he closed the door, he said, "I played piquet with Amsthorne."

This declaration caused her insides to knot, but she took a breath and continued to regard him. If he was smiling, then he surely could not have lost. However, Jasper—or rather, the Masked Rogue—had a reputation for never losing a game.

"I won," he announced, and her breath gushed, releasing the tension in her body. "But the momentary victory is not the reason for my good spirits but the recognition received at the club. I made some very useful acquaintances, and two of these gentlemen are willing to conduct business with me."

"Oh, George!" Natalie took both of his hands and smiled. "This is marvelous news!"

"Indeed!" Her cousin's grin was bright and unobstructed. "If all goes well, and I find someone willing to invest in the factory, then we would not have to sell the house and move to the country, Natalie." They would be closer to Hannah, too, if she married Wessberg.

The door opened at that instant, and Hannah walked in, her eyebrows furrowed. "George, did I hear you say, 'sell the house and move?'" His face colored ever so slightly while Natalie pressed her lips together. "Are you selling the house, Brother?" Hannah asked again, closing the door.

"Well, in light of our diminishing fortune, it is something Natalie and I considered," George replied.

Hannah turned to her. "You knew about this, Natalie?" She looked wounded, and Natalie suddenly felt guilty for not telling her.

"George and I did not tell you because we did not want you to worry, Hannah."

George cleared his throat. "Living in London is very expensive, and when Natalie and I discussed it, we thought it would be best to plan to move this winter." Hearing that, Hannah's frown deepened, but George was quick to continue elaborating. "We are hoping that our situation will change. I made some acquaintances that might benefit us."

"I'm not a child, Brother. You should have told me." Hannah seemed to be more bothered about not knowing than they thought. "After all, we must do what is necessary to live well."

Natalie began to understand the reason for her displeasure. She was a clever young woman who used her wit to earn and contribute to the household expenses. It was most unfair of Natalie and George to decide without her, even though it was for her benefit. As her lips parted to speak, Hannah turned and opened the door.

"We should have told her," George sighed, squeezing the bridge of his nose. "Why did we think that protecting her from this would be better?"

Natalie placed a comforting hand on his arm before following Hannah out. When she did not find her in any of the rooms downstairs, she checked her bedchamber. "Hannah, may I come in?" she asked after knocking.

She heard a sniffle before her cousin answered, and when she walked in, her heart fell at the sight of Hannah's eyes brimming with tears. Natalie quickly went to her and took her hands. "We wanted you to continue your search for a husband without worry. We see our mistake now, Hannah. Forgive us."

Her cousin wiped the lone tear that fell onto her cheek with her sleeve. "I understand, Natalie, and I appreciate your concern. If selling the house and moving will solve our problems, then I don't see any reason why we should not."

Hannah moved away from her and sat in a chair, blinking furiously to keep her tears from falling. Natalie thought there was another reason for her cousin's pain, and it might have a lot to do with Viscount Wessberg. Was Hannah in love with him? If the notion of being parted from him made her cry, then she might be.

What is keeping him from proposing?

Natalie knelt in front of her and took her hands again. "Everything is going to be all right, Hannah. Fate may yet look kindly upon us with George making acquaintances that could become business associates." Hannah nodded, but she did not look convinced, prompting Natalie to add, "We must always be bold enough to go after our hearts' desires."

That made Hannah sigh. "Thank you, Natalie."

"Of course."

Natalie left her, and on her way downstairs, she was stopped by the butler with a letter for her. "The messenger is awaiting a reply, My Lady," he informed her.

There was no imprint on the seal, but her heart stuttered the instant she opened it and began to read.

I SHALL BE WAITING FOR YOU AT ELEVEN O'CLOCK THREE NIGHTS FROM *today to grant your wish to gamble at a gentlemen's club.*

J.

SHE HURRIEDLY PENNED A REPLY AND HANDED IT TO THE BUTLER, and for the remainder of the day, anticipation and thoughts of Jasper distracted her.

NATALIE WAS LATE FOR DINNER, AND WHEN SHE WENT DOWN TO THE drawing room, she found George waiting alone. "Where is Hannah?"

George frowned. "I suppose she is late, or she does not wish to eat with us tonight after everything."

It was as they feared. Natalie was so excessively worried that she might skip dinner. "I will find her," she said decidedly, exiting the room and heading up to Hannah's bedchamber.

Her cousin was not in the bedchamber when she arrived, and Natalie was about to return to the drawing room when she looked behind her in the hallways and caught sight of her own bedchamber door open. Certain she had closed it earlier, she walked slowly toward it.

She pushed it open and walked inside. Hannah was standing near the bureau, reading what Natalie immediately recognized as the letter Jasper had sent her in the afternoon. Panic shot through her, and she dashed across the room to snatch the note from her cousin's hand.

"I came in looking for you so we may go down to dinner together, and when I saw this, I was too curious, and I..." Hannah trailed off, and a look of guilt shadowed her face. "I am sorry. I did not mean to pry."

Natalie watched her cousin to discern whether she knew the note was from Jasper, but nothing in her expression gave her a hint. Knowing Hannah very well, Natalie thought it would be better to tell her the truth. If she became more suspicious, she would ask more questions.

"We should go down to dinner," Natalie said, folding the note and placing it in a small drawer at the bureau.

"Yes." Hannah preceded her out of the room.

Dinner was quiet, but there was not as much tension as Natalie expected. In fact, Hannah's spirits appeared to have recovered. As soon as the meal was over and George retired to his study, Natalie led her cousin back to her bed chamber.

"I am sure you are curious," she began.

"Why would I not be, Natalie?" Hannah's eyes were wide, and she lowered her voice when she spoke again. "I never knew you wanted to gamble at a gentlemen's club."

"I have this list of things I want to do, experience before I am too old—"

"Fustian nonsense! One is never too old for anything."

Natalie laughed at that, feeling better about her plan to confide in her cousin. She never feared judgment from Hannah, but she must also be careful about what she revealed because she could not betray that Jasper was the Masked Rogue.

"Quite so. The Duke of Amsthorne has agreed to help me fulfill my wishes." As she revealed that, Hannah began to rock on the balls of her heels with excitement.

"The Duke?" she asked, but before Natalie could respond, she answered her own question. "The Duke! Oh, my goodness!"

"Be calm, Hannah!" Natalie giggled.

"Will he court you?"

"Oh, our arrangement is simpler than that." She took her cousin's hand and led her to sit by the window. "I no longer have the desire to marry." But a part of her still yearned for love. Her tenth wish might never be granted.

"What if you found a husband? Will you refuse him?"

"There are more pertinent matters to attend to, Hannah," Natalie replied, effectively changing the course of the conversation. "In three nights, I will join him to gamble at a gentlemen's club."

Hannah's excitement appeared to multiply by the moment. "How can I help you? I can purchase a mask for you to wear, and then you would be like the Masked Rogue. Oh, imagine The Londoner publishing a story about a female rogue about town! Society would go mad!"

"Hannah!" Natalie squeezed her hand to calm her, laughing.

"Oh," her cousin blushed. "I got lost, did I not?"

"Yes, you did," she said softly, patting Hannah's cheek. "I already have a mask and a white wig I intend to wear. I am also sewing a dress." She stood and walked over to a chair where the ivory satin she had obtained from Mary sat. She knew what she wanted to do with it now and the reason it had called to her at the shop. She picked the dress up and held it against her body to show Hannah.

"That is not yet a dress," Hannah observed with a tiny frown.

"I just cut it, but I can finish it in two days." She lowered the dress and picked up a sketchbook. "Here, I have a sketch."

When Hannah saw it, her mouth fell open. "Natalie, this is…" She stared at her in bewilderment. "Are *you* going to wear this?"

"Why not? It is one of my wishes."

Her cousin's grin was brighter than all the candles in the room. "Might I offer a suggestion?"

"Certainly."

"Lower the neckline. If the dress is to have this long a slit, then the neckline should be in agreement with the rest of it."

Natalie had not thought of that. When she cut the fabric, she decided to make a revealing dress to wear the same night she would gamble, and that would complete two wishes from her list. Now she could make the dress even more scandalous, and the Masked Rogue would be there with her to live up to every forbidden moment.

She found a pencil, and together, they resketched, making something incredibly glamorous.

"I will be barely clothed in this, Hannah," Natalie said conspiratorially.

"Yes, a gentlewoman should never wear this, but that is what makes this perfect. For one night, you could leave everything behind and be anything you desire."

Indeed, she quietly agreed, *for one night, I could truly be me.*

Chapter Fifteen

London has seen yet another uneventful night. It is as though the Masked Rogue is hiding after the destruction his nocturnal adventure had wrought. Or is he planning something that would shock the wigs off our heads? Our eyes are open, London, and we are seated on the edges of our chairs, breathless with anticipation.

Hannah pinned Natalie's red hair before placing the large white wig that weighed more than a wig ever should. "Is this how the French court carried this thing?" Natalie complained.

"Oh, yes. You could decide not to wear it, though. No one will recognize you with the powder and the demi-mask."

"Yes, but my hair is red, and there are not many women with red hair. Most wear wigs."

"Especially for the Masked Rogue," Hannah laughed. "Do you think he would notice you if he saw you tonight?"

"I doubt he would be at a gentlemen's club."

"What if he made an exception tonight?"

"I doubt he would." Natalie drew her face away when Hannah raised the powder puff, shaking her head. "I do not want that. I have enough heavy things on me."

"Very well." Hannah started toward the door. "I shall be back shortly."

Natalie regarded herself in the mirror, her stomach fluttering with nerves. Something told her that tonight, the very course of her existence would change, and even though she did not know how, she embraced it.

Her cousin returned with a black box that she set down at Natalie's feet. A gasp escaped her when the box was opened, and she saw the most beautiful black wool cloak. It was lined with fur, and the hem was embroidered with gold thread in delicate patterns that swirled.

"Hannah, where did you get this?"

"I thought you would need it tonight. Instead of accepting money for the story I submitted yesterday, I requested the cloak, which I saw through the window of a shop on Picadilly."

"This is wonderful!" Natalie hugged her. "Still, you shouldn't have done that."

"Oh, but I have selfish intentions," Hannah said as she pulled away. "If you look delectable tonight, the Duke might just marry you."

Natalie let out a nervous laugh. "Are you asking me to seduce him?"

"I do not believe you have to. Everything you have on should do the work."

Natalie had planned on wearing her old cloak, but now that she had this one, she could not be more grateful to Hannah. Her emotions rose as a result, and she swallowed against the tide, determined to smile and make the most of the night she had. "Thank you!"

"What would you do without me, hmm, Natalie?" Hannah teased, and they laughed before Hannah helped her into the cloak.

THE RAKISH DUKE AND HIS SPINSTER

It was almost eleven, and the household—which now consisted only of a maid, a footman, and the butler—was quiet, as her cousin helped her sneak out.

Once she was outside through the servants' entrance, she looked about the alley, and at the end to her right was a black carriage that was barely visible in the night. She suspected it was Jasper's, and she made her way to it.

A man wearing a dark cloak and a wide-brimmed hat stepped down from the carriage and walked toward her. She smiled as she recognized him.

JASPER WAS NERVOUS. FOR THE FIRST TIME IN HIS LIFE, HE FELT HIS palms dampen in his black leather gloves and his neckcloth uncomfortably tight. His heart also beat frantically as he walked toward Natalie. Despite it all, a smile stole onto his features when he stopped in front of her.

Saying nothing, he found her hand and led her quickly to the carriage. The cold was biting, but more than that, they should not be seen. Smith was driving them tonight. Jasper always rode when he was the Masked Rogue, but he had company tonight, and the only man he could trust was his valet. The carriage had no crest to identify him, and the interior was dark. He'd had it made for when the Masked Rogue needed it.

Natalie looked ridiculous in a white wig and a mask that did not conceal as much of her face as it ought to. Once they were settled in the carriage, and it had begun to move, he moved to sit beside her on the front-facing seat. "Good evening," he murmured, his eyes moving to her hands that clutched the lapels of her cloak tightly. She seemed to be as nervous as he was, if not more.

She returned his greeting, but she did not release the cloak. Jasper grew incredibly curious to know what she was hiding. To begin unraveling her, he said, "I want you free tonight, and this wig might be a hindrance."

Her eyes widened. One of the carriage lamps was near the window, and it shone some light onto her. They could not be seen from outside, however. "My hair is red, Jasper."

"I know." *Oh, he knew that more than she could ever imagine.* "May I?"

A tiny sly smile curved her lips. "You may remove it if you can dress my hair."

"Trust me," he whispered, inching closer to her, both her natural scent and the perfume she wore driving his senses into an intoxicating frenzy. When she allowed him, he gently lifted the large wig from her head and set it down, and then he removed the mask.

"What are you doing?" she asked, alarmed.

"I thought you agreed to trust me?"

"You are revealing me."

Every word out of her mouth tonight was a message of temptation, and he chuckled, shifting slightly in his seat. Her hazel eyes appeared amber tonight, and her soft lips were begging him to be kissed.

Jasper removed the pins from her hair, murmuring, "Tonight, you are not Lady Natalie Reeves, but—"

She placed a finger against his lips. "I know who I am tonight." She said that with such confidence that he blinked at her. He had wanted to say that she was the Masked Rogue's lady, but looking at her at this very moment, he was glad she stopped him. He wanted to claim her as Jasper and not his alter ego.

"Very well." He continued removing the pins, sending her red curls tumbling down seductively. "Let your locks frame your face and add to the disguise."

"I will wear my mask," she insisted, and he laughed.

"You will wear your mask," he reassured her, reaching for the cloak.

"You do not want to see this now, Jasper," she warned, holding the edges tighter.

"What are you hiding?" He was more intrigued than ever.

"I cannot show you now."

"Why?" He held her slight shoulders. "I implore you, Natalie. Whatever it is, I think you should show me."

"You will not send me back to my house to change. Promise me that."

Now Jasper was certain she was dressed in something she was not supposed to, and it heated his blood. "You have my word."

Slowly, she parted the cloak and let it fall from her shoulders. Jasper stopped breathing. The ivory dress she had on was the most enticing thing he had ever seen a woman wear. "Holy God, Natalie!" he swore.

The neckline was very low, enough to reveal the lovely mounds of her breasts, and there were barely any sleeves on the dress, only a trim of lace. The bodice clung to her tiny waist and flared at her hips. As his eyes moved down, his erection grew painful. Not only was the skirt not full, but it also had a long slit that stopped at her thigh, showing the black stockings she wore. This woman was seduction personified, and Jasper had already lost any game she played before it started.

He had made her a promise too early because now he did not want any other man to see her thus. Jasper wanted her all to himself. He pulled the cloak over her shoulders. "I am not covering you because I am displeased. I am doing so to preserve myself from your charm."

She giggled, and he raised his eyes to hers. Unable to stop himself, he removed his mask and took her face between his palms, claiming her lips. Her little sigh undid him, and he wrapped an arm around her waist, pulling her to him, her breasts pressing softly against his chest.

Why did she have to be a Goddess? And why am I only meeting her now, when

I am at the end of my journey? This thought pained him so much that he found the will to let her go.

"If your intention is to disarm me with desire tonight, Natalie. I must say that you have succeeded."

"Wearing this dress is another item on my list," she revealed, and he cocked his head, fascinated. At the same time, he was aching inside and tempted to have the carriage turned so he could take her back to his manor instead. "I did not wear it for you." She might as well have because she had won almost every part of him over.

Jasper felt his lips curl in a sly smile. Her retorts were as delightful as she was. Natalie covered herself and regarded him defiantly.

"Where are we going?" she asked. "The Masked Rogue scarcely visits gentlemen's clubs."

"There is one I have in mind tonight. It is obscure, and your identity would be safer there." Jasper returned to the rear-facing seat, willing his body to behave. She had the power to turn him mindless with lust, and he did not want to kiss her again before they reached their destination.

The remainder of the trip was spent in savory banter, and Jasper found himself almost wishing that they would never arrive. It was a sweet torture, with his senses yearning and his mind enjoying her witty response to every comment he made.

They arrived at last, and Jasper found himself oddly reluctant to leave the carriage. He reached into the box on the seat beside him and removed the mask he had fashioned for her. "Wear this. It will conceal your face better."

Her eyes enlarged at the sight of the mask. The gold edges matched the trimmings of her dress, and the ivory satin was made just for her. "This is beautiful, Jasper."

"It can never compare to you," he whispered without thinking, and only when she looked at him, did he realize what he had said. The delightful color on her cheeks told him that she was pleased. Natalie wore the mask and fluffed her lustrous hair, then he wore his mask and alighted the carriage before helping her down.

The night could now begin, and only the heavens knew how it would end.

Chapter Sixteen

❦

Sinful rakes and witless dandies. We have their escapades to report since we are being starved by the Masked Rogue. Our search beyond London is as fruitless as the Marquess of Kinsdale's marriage, and we are losing confidence.

Jasper and Natalie were shown into a salon decorated in deep shades of red and brown. This club allowed women, but only those of questionable reputations, and their purpose was to entertain the gentlemen. Natalie was not to be anyone's entertainment, however, and Jasper held her close to him.

When he removed her cloak and handed it to the footman who showed them to the salon, the poor man's eyes bulged, and he swallowed, quickly looking away when he met Jasper's cold glare. Bowing hastily, he excused them.

They were alone in the room, and he took her hand to lead her to a table on one end as she asked, "Do you come here often? The footman seems familiar with you."

Jasper's brows rose immediately as he caught her French accent. It was accurate, too. Her disguise was not merely in appearance, and he loved it. A smile curved one corner of his mouth. "This is the only club the Rogue would deign to visit."

"Deign, *Monsieur?*" Natalie raised a sultry eyebrow, and as he lowered her into a red velvet chair, he leaned over her.

"*Oui, mademoiselle,*" he returned. "You never told me your name."

"I am the *Comtesse Jacqueline De Villepin,*" she replied, her eyes sparkling in the candlelight.

Jasper took her hand and kissed it. "I am delighted to make your acquaintance, Comtesse." He admired her clever title, and there was a daring innocence about her that moved him to make her his. This feeling was more than lust, and it was more than the magic of the night. He quickly pushed it away and got onto one knee, and then he started tugging her black satin glove down her arm.

"Oh, *Monsieur,* you are being very impatient tonight. Will you not wait until we have returned to your ship?"

Apparently, they were lovers, and he lived on a ship. Excellent story to make London lose its mind. "You make me mad with lust, *Comtesse,*" he growled, relishing every minute of their game. He kissed her bare arm, abstractedly noticing that her fingers were slightly rough. "I can never have enough of you."

Natalie giggled, and one of her hands raked his hair, sliding down the side of his face to touch the mouth of the mask. "*Non, Monsieur.* We must wait." She looked past his shoulders, and he saw her tense almost imperceptibly. "Besides, we have company."

Jasper turned to see Baron Peckhart in the doorway, and his dark eyes were on Natalie. More specifically, on her bosom. "Mr. Rogue," he said, walking into the room. "Fancy seeing you here tonight."

"You as well, Baron," Jasper said through a tight jaw, rising to face the Baron and barring his path to Natalie.

"Who is that delectable creature you are hiding, Mr. Rogue?" Peckhart's eyes gleamed.

"Comtesse De Villepin," Natalie said behind him, holding her hand to the Baron.

Damn it!

"Oh, a countess!" Baron Peckhart knelt in front of her and kissed the hand that Natalie had just exposed. "Are you a real one?" he inquired.

Natalie rolled her eyes and called him an adorable fool in French. Of course, he did not understand and continued grinning and drooling over her. Jasper placed a hand on his shoulder.

"That is quite enough, Baron. The Comtesse is mine." When Peckhart lingered, Jasper drew him to his feet. "Did you not hear what I said?" he growled.

Peckhart swallowed. "Indeed, I have."

Releasing him, Jasper walked over to Natalie and took her hand, pulling her up. Then he sat in her chair and placed her on his lap, wrapping possessive arms around her small waist.

"What if I play you for a moment for her?" Peckhart asked, and Jasper almost shot to his feet and pounded his face. How dare he assume he could have her? But he reminded himself that Natalie was not a lady tonight but a daring Comtesse. Every man in this establishment was certain to lust after her.

She spoke before he could say anything to defend her. "I am not a piece to be won, Baron. I am particular about my company, and I will have you know that I chose the Rogue tonight and not the contrary." Peckhart was flustered by that response, and she dealt him another blow when she said, "Besides, an undefeated champion is superior company."

Peckhart glared at Jasper while he grinned in triumph. In a blatant display of power, he kissed Natalie's shoulder with the artificial mouth on his mask, and she sucked in her breath, gazing down at him.

"*Naughty, Monsieur!*"

He laughed and pulled her tighter against him. Four gentlemen entered the room then, all stopping the instant they laid eyes on her. Peckhart found a seat in a corner while the gentlemen hovered curiously.

"That is the Countess De Villepin," the Baron told them. "The Rogue won't let you near her. He has his teeth into her like a wolf."

"It is *Comtesse*, Baron," Natalie corrected with affected vivacity, and the gentlemen laughed at him. One of them bowed in Natalie's direction.

"A pleasure, Comtesse."

She turned back to Jasper without acknowledging him, and again, victory coursed through his veins. More gentlemen poured into the room, all hungry for an introduction to the Goddess, and he refused to grant each of them.

"Fancy a round of whist, Rogue?" One gentleman asked. "Or are you here to show us your lady?"

"We do," Natalie answered for them. The gentleman seemed to balk, but two others, Mr. Lupton and Lord Phelps, rose and took his place, coming to the table.

"We would be delighted to play a round with you, Comtesse," Mr. Lupton said in a charming tone while his eyes roamed her body.

"I do not believe I have ever seen you around," Phelps said to Natalie as Jasper began to shuffle the cards.

"Why would you see me?" she responded with a sardonic rise of her eyebrow. "I am only in England for this man," she added, a sultry smile spreading across her lips.

Jasper smiled. He wanted to kiss her in front of these men to seal her words, but it would require the removal of their masks. He looked at Phelps and dealt him his cards first, challenging him to respond to Natalie's statement. Of course, he could not. Like most of the foolish fops about town, he waved his title about like a flag with no substantial wit to support it.

"Well then, I hope we will see you more often now that the Rogue has deigned to show his gem to us," Lupton said as he received his cards.

"Oh, but a gem is hardly one if everyone could see it as they please," Natalie smirked. Jasper tugged slightly at his neckcloth in an effort to contain the laugh bubbling in his chest. It was evident that people around had caught on to Natalie's subtle insults, and they were all trying to hide their mirth, too.

"You never told me that you spoke French," he whispered in her ear, and he placed her cards in her hand.

"The night is full of surprises, no?" She rose from his lap and sat on one corner of the table. "And you may not have a peek at my cards, *Monsieur*." He was starting to love the way she called him that. Lupton swallowed thirstily at her closeness, and Jasper gave him a warning look.

They began to play, and it quickly became apparent that Clifford was not the only one skilled at cards in the family. She quickly outplayed Lupton and Phelps, and when it was only the two of them left, he wondered if she would win.

Jasper surprised himself by allowing her to win. This was not a night to stroke his ego. She might not appreciate the fact that he allowed her to win, but he could not bring himself to compete with her before all these men.

Lupton and Phelps kissed her knuckles in congratulations, and this did not please Jasper. He gently drew her back onto his lap and asked if anyone was interested in another game. "Only with the Comtesse," he said.

"You will not play?" she asked, surprised.

"You are on a victorious path, and I wish for you to stay upon it."

He placed a large wager for her, and they played. With every victory, she made an excited little jump that engorged his member while her bosom danced delectably underneath her dress, the candlelight casting a soft glow upon it.

Jasper noticed everyone staring shamelessly at Natalie, and bitterness tightened his throat. Acting entirely on impulse, he rose and took her hand, leading her across the room to the door. Although her surprise was apparent in her lovely eyes, she neither stopped nor protested. He made his way to the private room that was always reserved for him and guided her inside, locking the door.

"Why did you do that?" Natalie looked utterly displeased by his interruption of their game. He also found it impressive that she could hide her displeasure from everyone else.

"Perhaps you should ask yourself that, or the gentlemen," he returned, something uncomfortable burning in his chest. He knew he was being irrational at the moment, but he could not help himself.

"I do not see anything wrong with their pleasant reception of us," she argued.

"I see *everything* wrong with it." His voice was too passionate.

Natalie started to speak but stopped. "Are you perhaps...jealous?" She sounded amused now, and he wished he could see all of her face.

If that is what the bitterness I am feeling is, then I am jealous. Incomprehensibly so. None of those gentlemen had the right to regard her the way they did.

You have no right, as well, a small mocking voice pointed out in his mind, but Jasper snuffed it, pulling her into his arms before she could put in any more words and taking her mouth in a searing kiss.

Chapter Seventeen

Ladies and gentlemen, the Masked Rogue of London lives on a ship! Now we may search every ship at the harbor for his abode.

Jasper kissed Natalie thoroughly, holding her against a wall and covering her body with his. He removed both of their masks and tossed them onto the floor.

She never imagined he would be jealous, but the discovery strengthened her confidence, and since she was a different woman tonight, she wanted to gain pleasure.

"You are mine, Natalie," Jasper murmured as he feathered kisses along her neck, moving down to her breasts.

She caught his face and raised it so she could look into his eyes. "I am not yours," she said, because if she allowed him to continue to pronounce it, she might feel and even hope it would be real. Natalie wanted to spare herself that trouble. "But the Comtesse could be, though."

His eyes darkened, and he cupped her posterior with one hand, squeezing enticingly. "I can accept that." He returned his mouth to her neck while she unfastened the three buttons at the back of her dress. All he needed was to feel it give before he pulled it down her body very slowly, and his mouth descended with the fabric.

Natalie closed her eyes and leaned against the wall, her breath hitching and her body tightening with need. Her nights had been filled with torrid dreams of Jasper satiating her hunger, finishing what they had begun in the garden. Her hands clutched his hair when his mouth closed over one breast and suckled. Despite being familiar with the pleasure, it took her this time as if she had never felt it before, winding her nerves and creating sweet knots in her belly. Her sex, which had been throbbing all evening, grew more insistent, and she felt the warm moisture dribble to her thighs.

"Jasper," she moaned, rolling her eyes in wanton craving, "I...I...need you."

He raised his head and grinned at her, his hand replacing his mouth at her nipple and continuing the sensual punishment. "*Je sais, ma cherié.* You will have everything you desire soon." He drew her dress the rest of the way and stood back, his eyes flaring as he regarded her. "You are divine."

She wore nothing but a flimsy petticoat that she had made to cling to her legs. It had a slit too. His gaze washed her with more need, and she clenched her teeth. "Don't torture me!"

Jasper laughed devilishly. "I would not dream of it." He scooped her up and took her to a divan. As he lowered her into it, his hands roamed her body, pulling the petticoat down. He removed her black satin shoes when he reached her feet and tossed everything to the floor, then he lowered himself onto his knees and began to kiss her ankle, rolling her stockings down as his mouth moved up.

Her body trembled, and Natalie thought she would perish before he touched her where she yearned for him the most. Even as she grasped his hair and continued to mewl and writhe, he kissed her legs slowly, determined to protract the moment for as long as he was able.

"Jasper," she gasped.

"Hmm?"

"I will...return this...punishment." She arched her back when he kissed the soft skin on the inside of her thigh, parting her legs for him. "Mark..." Breathing was becoming laborious. "Mar... Oh, Jasper!"

She pushed against his shoulders when his mouth found her center, but it was not to push him away. He understood the encouragement and buried his face between her thighs, kissing her so deeply she quivered, feeling every sensation at once. The pleasure quickly rose, and the climax she had dreamed of since he touched her in the gardens at the ball returned. But before it could take her, he pulled away from her.

Natalie protested, the sound of a tiny sob from her lips. "Hold on, darling," he rasped, urgently taking off his coat and waistcoat. His boots and shirt followed, revealing a body so spectacularly sculpted, he could be a marble god. His mouth curving into a teasing smirk, he pulled his breeches down his legs.

Her breath caught, and she sat up, marveling at his anatomy. Her body responded with more longing, and when he returned to her, he placed himself between her legs and took himself in hand, touching the tip of his member to her sex. She shivered and wrapped one leg around his waist, and he pressed against her bud, rolling and stealing every last thread of her senses that was left. Her head fell back as a hundred different sensations hit her like waves. She knew they could find pleasure without him entering her, but she was surprised at the measure.

He leaned forward and kissed her lips, and that sent her spiraling into sensual chaos. Tiny stars formed at the back of her eyes, and her whole body shook with the force of her gratification. One of his arms went around her waist to hold her against his chest while he moved his pelvis away from hers and continued stroking himself.

Jasper cooed in her ear and feathered kisses on her dewy temples. She took as much air as she could into her lungs, and when her body began to calm, she reached between them to curl her fingers around his member. His body jerked, and he groaned her name.

Jasper thrust his pelvis as she moved her hand up and down. His skin was incredibly smooth and velvety, and he seemed to enlarge in her hand. "Show me what to do," she whispered.

He covered her hand with his and stroked faster, his lips parting, his eyes growing heavy, and a vein appearing on his neck. He was alluringly masculine, and Natalie raised her chin for another kiss.

The heated union of their lips was quickly rivaled by the hardening of his manhood. Every inch of him was rigid, and he moved her hand more fiercely until he attained the height of his pleasure. Groaning, he broke their kiss and rested his forehead in the crook of her shoulder.

Natalie felt triumphant, but more than that, she felt an inexplicable closeness to him. When he raised his head to look at her, she swallowed nervously, trying not to let her emotions be seen.

"My God, Natalie," he murmured, stroking her cheek. "You are ruining me." He seemed to have abandoned the Comtesse.

You have already ruined me for any other man, she wanted to say. No one could compare to him now. In fact, she could never allow anyone to. In response, she smiled and nipped his jaw with her teeth, causing him to laugh.

"Now, then, you were saying something about a *mark*," he reminded her, and she had to think to remember what it was.

"I was going to say, *mark my words*," she completed. "You will feel every divine torture you subjected me to, Jasper."

"I am counting upon it," he chuckled, moving to the other end of the divan and pulling her with him such that they were seated and in each other's arms.

"Does anyone know we are here?" she asked.

"Yes." Jasper languidly stroked her arm while she rested her head against his shoulder.

"Do they know what we did?"

"It is no business of theirs." He placed a finger beneath her chin and raised her face to his. "Natalie. May I ask you a favor?"

"What do you want?" Her eyes fluttered when he brought his lips close to hers.

"Do not make me bring you to such a place again. You can never know how difficult it was for me to see those men regard you as though you were a demimonde."

She smiled, pleased with how protective of her he was. "I will not come here again. I do not like being regarded thusly, but I have fulfilled my wish."

"Excellent." He kissed her, then began to stroke her body all over again, reigniting the passionate embers with her.

It was past four in the morning when Jasper helped her dress. "Do you think London will talk about us in the morning?" she asked as he rolled a stocking up her leg, while she untangled her hair with her fingers.

"Believe me, darling, society has found a new obsession." He looked up at her. "They will not let you go now."

She grinned. "It is unfortunate that I will not wear this mask again."

"Do not be too certain about that," he murmured. "I am not letting you or Comtesse De Villepin leave me."

Her heart raced at the pronouncement, even though she was yet to discern his meaning. That hope she had been trying to smother was maturing, and it frightened her.

Chapter Eighteen

Comtesse Jacqueline De Villepin. That is the name the mysterious lady identified with. Like the Rogue she kept company, she wore a mask that no one dared to question. She has also managed to turn every gentleman's brain into mush, both those who encountered her and those absent. Her name is the only word on their lips, and their wives, fiancées, and ladies are beginning to wag their tongues in protest.

It was almost dawn when Jasper returned to the manor. He had kissed Natalie for a wonderful half hour in the carriage when they stopped at her house, and now he was quite bereft without her.

He was pleased, however—more than he had been in a long while. He quietly hummed to himself as he moved through the manor, and when he reached his bedchamber, he removed his coat and boots before flopping onto the bed and sleeping.

His body had not felt this manner of bliss in years, and he slept through most of the morning. When he was awake, Smith brought his breakfast up to his chambers.

At noon, he went to one of the drawing rooms to find Phoebe, and when he walked in, stifling a yawn, his aunt gave him a look.

"What seems to have robbed you of sleep?" She quirked a dubious brow.

"Business," Jasper lied shamelessly, the image of Natalie's glorious body playing in his thoughts.

"I see," Phoebe said. She was thankfully distracted by the gossip sheet she was scanning through, otherwise, he was certain that she would press him for answers. "Society is still talking about your dance with Lady Natalie." She handed him the gossip sheet. "It is too cold to walk in the park, but you could ride along Rotten Row with her for a short while. It is unfortunate that this is not the season of romance."

Jasper bit back a smile. This was the exact season for romance. Alas, it was not for him. Asking Natalie to the park would only give her the wrong message and further fuel society's gossip. Their secret arrangement was quite enough, and he had found a measure of peace through it. In her company, he forgot his impending demise.

However, Jasper found a part of him wondering if it truly was enough. He quickly schooled his thoughts when he realized the dangerous direction they were headed, and he read The Londoner. It was talking about Comtesse De Villepin and the Masked Rogue.

"I do not see my name and Lady Natalie's," he said.

"Oh, it is the final paragraph. The Rogue and his mistress might have stolen all the attention, but society did not forget about you." His aunt grinned, and her blue eyes sparkled.

Now, IN SPITE OF THIS NEW DEVELOPMENT, WE WOULD LIKE TO REMIND *you of courtship expectations that are building. Many believe the Duke of Amsthorne is finally seeking a wife, and he might have found it in dear Lady Natalie Reeves. Should we expect a wedding this winter?*

. . .

An idea suddenly came to Jasper as he read that last paragraph. It was one bound to quiet his aunt and have her leave him be with regard to matchmaking. "Aunt Phoebe, what do you think about hosting a soiree? Right here in the manor. Lady Natalie and her family shall be the first to receive our invitation, of course."

"Excellent!" His aunt gave a delighted clap of her hands. "I shall see to the preparations at once." She hopped off her seat and walked out of the room, calling the butler, Wayne.

Jasper anticipated seeing Natalie again, and a soiree seemed like a perfect excuse. He was in search of a lot of those lately, he realized. He was doing everything to see her.

Natalie opened her eyes to Hannah staring back at her. She bolted upright and clutched the duvet to her chest, but then she remembered that she was clothed. Her cheeks colored with the memory of last night's events.

"It took you long to wake up," Hannah whispered.

"Never say you were waiting for me to wake up so that you may question me about last night," Natalie yawned.

"You are fortunate I did not wake you up," her cousin grinned. "I deserve compensation for my patience." She sat on the bed and regarded Natalie with large, curious eyes.

"You will be rewarded by the Divine for your patience, not me," she giggled.

"So, what happened last night?"

Hannah had been asleep when Natalie returned. She had also won two thousand pounds, which she claimed before leaving the club. Of course, a hundred guineas out of the sum would be repaid to Jasper, for he placed the first wager for her. This money would help them greatly, but she was not going to reveal it to George just yet. He would want to know where exactly she had obtained the sum from. She would have to think of what to tell him first.

Now she tried to rub the sleep from her face to answer her cousin's questions. "It was splendid." She rose from the bed.

"That is no answer," Hannah protested, following her and stopping on the other side of the screen while Natalie filled a basin with water and splashed it on her face.

"I played a good game with several gentlemen."

"Where did you go?"

"A club on Coventry Street." She dried her face and began to clean her teeth.

"Dale's?" Hannah asked.

Natalie never went to the trouble of knowing which club it was. When they arrived, she was consumed by her nerves, and when they left, she was eager to climb into the carriage and be out from the cold. She also wanted Jasper's arms around her, and he was all too happy to oblige.

"Err...yes, that one," she answered, then went on to tell Hannah how enjoyable the night had been and what games she played. She was careful not to reveal anyone's name because it would give Hannah a hint about the Rogue. She was sure his name and the Comtesse's were in the Londoner already.

When she dressed and emerged from the screen, she saw an odd look on her cousin's face—something akin to suspicion—but it disappeared quickly with Hannah saying, "I think the Duke is fond of you, Natalie. I read the Londoner this morning, and you two were mentioned again."

"Do not be silly, Hannah," Natalie dismissed, her cheeks warming again. "...What else was in the Londoner?" she asked, curious about the tale of the Comtesse that was undoubtedly being carried about.

Hannah shrugged. "Nothing of note."

Natalie's eyes narrowed as she grew suspicious of her cousin. Hannah knew something about the Masked Rogue and the Comtesse, and she was not telling her.

She confirmed it when she found a copy of the Londoner on a table near the door. The paper gushed about them, yet Hannah pretended she had read nothing. She likely wrote the piece, too.

※

That afternoon, Hannah joined Natalie as they left for Mary's shop to deliver some of Phoebe's finished dresses, and Alexandra was examining one of the dresses that were made for her when they entered.

"I rather liked the dress Lady Phoebe wore to the Countess of Devonham's musicale last week. I should like something in a similar style," Alexandra said to Mary. The particular dress had been another of Natalie's works.

Mary's gaze met Natalie's through the mirror before Alexandra, and her friend gave her a knowing smile. A snicker escaped Hannah at Alexandra's demand, drawing the attention of the lady in question. Hannah was laughing because Alexandra despised Natalie, yet wanted the dresses she made. She would no doubt call them ugly if she knew the truth.

Alexandra stepped off the low stool she was on and walked to where they were standing, glaring at Hannah. To their surprise, she did not say anything to her. Instead, she focused her contemptuous attention on Natalie.

"Do you know what rumor I heard, Lady Natalie?" Alexandra began.

"I cannot imagine," Natalie drawled, causing Hannah to hold a laugh.

Alexandra fleetingly scowled at this, but she tried to maintain her smugness, and she leaned close to Natalie and whispered, "Society is beginning to believe that your unmarried state is the result of a scandal years ago."

Panic rose within her, and her hands tightened around the beaded string of her reticule. She breathed evenly and did all she could to appear unperturbed. No one knew about those details but her father, cousins, and the man behind it all, Oliver, who was not even in the country. How could Alexandra have known?

Oliver had hidden Jasper's name when he extorted her family. So, apart from Natalie and Oliver, no one else knew that it was Jasper with her that night. If George had known that it was Jasper, he would have challenged him, and he would not have agreed to play a game with him at White's.

"Is that so?" Natalie asked calmly. "Did The Londoner publish that tale?"

Alexandra's mouth twisted with disdain. "I do not read that nonsense."

Hannah began to counter, but Natalie stopped her. She did not want her involved in this bickering. "Is society so starved of proper occupation that I am now its subject of gossip and speculation?" When she asked that, Mary held her laugh while Hannah was positively shaking with mirth.

What was even more unfortunately humorous was the fact that Alexandra was still oblivious to the fact that Natalie had just implied that *she* was the society and that she was so concerned with Natalie's life that she would speak to anyone about her. Hannah had heard that Alexandra had tea with some ladies two days ago, and all she talked about was Natalie and how unfortunate her spinsterhood was.

Alexandra sniffed, trying to appear unbothered by what Natalie had just said. She turned to Hannah and jabbed a finger in her direction, saying, "You! If you think that Viscount you are trailing after is going to offer for you, then you must be gravely delusional. Once served, men hardly ever look at a woman again. They use, and then they discard. It is in their nature, you see."

This comment promptly removed the smile on Hannah's face. Natalie quickly stepped forward to defend her cousin. "I do not believe you are in any position to say that, Miss Gilmore. Unless you wish for us to discuss the four gentlemen that courted you without making you an offer."

"I did receive—"

"Everyone knows they did not offer for you," Natalie interjected. "Before you cast your judgment upon others, think first of your situation."

Alexandra's face contorted before she snatched up her reticule from a chair and walked out of the shop.

"The only reason I tolerate her is that she purchases a new dress every week," Mary sighed upon Alexandra's exit. "If I had my way, I would choose who patronizes me."

For the remainder of the afternoon, Alexandra's words about the scandal and that being the reason for Natalie's spinsterhood plagued her. She gave Mary Phoebe's dress and returned home with Hannah.

George found them in the drawing room with an invitation, which he held up, a smile on his face. "We have a soirée to attend at the Duke of Amsthorne's residence."

Natalie's insides tightened with anticipation. They had never been invited to any event hosted by Jasper or Phoebe. Their family lacked society's favor because of their debts. Until now.

"I *told* you, Natalie," Hannah cried, running up to George and taking the invitation from him, "The Duke is fond of you!"

"Hannah!" Natalie reprimanded.

"Did you just say that Amsthorne is fond of Natalie, Hannah?" George inquired, his eyes widening with interest. She groaned because she did not want him to have false hopes with regard to her marriage. They had already accepted that she would never marry.

"Sorry," Hannah mouthed to Natalie.

"Do not mind her, George," Natalie dismissed. "Society is carrying around a rumor. Pay it no mind, please."

"Yes, it is nothing of consequence, George," Hannah supported.

"Amsthorne having potential interest in you is not a matter to be disregarded, Natalie," George responded. "And remember, I do have cause to believe Hannah. Surely getting an invitation for the first time from him after dancing with you holds something more."

"Perhaps my friendship with Lady Phoebe is behind all of this," Natalie murmured in an attempt to draw him away from being hopeful.

"No." George shook his head. "The Duke would not have danced with you simply because you are friends with Lady Phoebe."

"George," Natalie's voice was forceful, "the Duke is just an acquaintance."

"Very well, Natalie. If you say so." He finally acquiesced. Natalie was beginning to calm down when he suddenly added, "You shall have a new dress for the upcoming soiree. Both of you. No objections." He looked sternly from her to Hannah, who smirked like a fox.

Natalie had no choice but to accept this. She did, however, make a mental note to secretly supplement even more into their accounts from her wins. George wanted her to have a new dress to impress Jasper because, like many others, he was hoping for a match between them. Nothing she did stopped him.

The expectation that now rested upon her shoulders was too great, and she wanted to tell someone that she could not marry Jasper. He would never offer for her. And he was the man who compromised her a decade ago.

Chapter Nineteen

The Comtesse with fiery hair and emerald green eyes had London under her spell. Some gentlemen swear they had never beheld a more beautiful creature, especially Mr. Lupton and Baron Peckhart. We apologize to the Baron's poor wife if she is reading this. Comtesse De Villepin claimed that she came to England only to be with the Masked Rogue. Could she be the woman he rescued at Hyde Park? Is he in love with her?

Jasper was at Whites again when he spied Clifford poring over the contents of a sheet. He joined him at his table but had to clear his throat to get the Earl's attention.

"My apologies, Your Grace." Clifford set aside the paper.

"Please, call me Jasper or Amsthorne," he said. He rather liked the Earl and did not mind friendship with him. The little time he had left also made him disdain formality.

"I shall call you Amsthorne then," Clifford agreed with a small smile.

Jasper glanced at the sheet on the table. "I did not know you read The Londoner earnestly."

"Do we not all?" Clifford chuckled. "It is telling us more about the Comtesse."

Jasper sucked in his breath. No one knew who the Comtesse was, and he was glad that Natalie would not wear the mask again or go out in public in that seductive dress. He had already given Smith the task of covering anything good enough to expose her, as he did for himself.

Two gentlemen walked into the salon at that moment, and they were talking about the Comtesse. Jasper's jaw clenched as he wondered when the obsession would cease. He had guessed correctly when he told Natalie that they would not let her go. He had to do what must be done to protect her, and maybe he needed to set some measures in place to shield her should the situation overpower Smith. After all, he would be leaving soon, and when he did, she might be exposed.

"Are you well, Amsthorne?" Clifford asked, and Jasper blinked.

"I am well. Never mind my distraction. Did you say something?"

"I was asking if you would accept a challenge to play a game against the Rogue?"

"Perhaps I have already played the Rogue," Jasper responded slyly.

"I beg your pardon?" Clifford's brows furrowed.

"With your unmatched skill, you could be the Masked Rogue for all I know," Jasper added to turn any suspicion Clifford might have around.

The Earl burst out laughing at this. "Oh, believe me, if I were the Masked Rogue of London, my identity would have been out by now."

"Why do you say that," Jasper asked.

"Well, I have two very curious sisters. They would have found my mask."

Jasper admired him for thinking of Natalie as his sister instead of his cousin. He had become too concerned about her, and he was seeking ways for her to be comfortable and lack for nothing after he was gone. He had also pondered the reason her hands were rough. A lady's hands ought to be the softest, yet Natalie's spoke of a hidden toil.

Her family's financial situation could explain it, but Jasper still struggled with it. What did she do to earn an income?

Jasper sent for Smith the minute he returned to the manor, and the valet met him in his study.

"The masks I had made, I want you to have several more made. About five pairs—half for the Rogue and half for the Comtesse. Then place them upon ships in the harbor."

Smith's grin was positively evil when he bowed. "It will be done, Your Grace." It would effectively mislead people. "I have a message for you," Smith added. At Jasper's encouraging nod, he said, "The Earl of Clifford intends to sell his townhouse on Berkeley Square."

Jasper tensed. "Has his situation worsened to the point of selling his home?"

"It would appear so, Your Grace."

Jasper thought for a minute before instructing, "Have my solicitor meet me in the morning."

"At once, Your Grace. Will that be all?"

"Yes."

As Smith opened the door to leave, Oliver Bargrave walked into the room. Jasper momentarily ignored his worries and stood with a broad smile, skirting his desk to meet his dearest friend.

"Oliver, you devil!" Jasper clapped his friend on the back.

"You ought to call me Ecklehill now," Oliver teased. He came into his title a year ago when his grandfather, the former Earl, died.

"Well then, Ecklehill, I thought you would only deign to set foot on English soil after my hair has grown silver and my face wrinkled."

"Should I go back and return when you are silver and wrinkled?" Oliver laughed.

A tiny voice sought to remind Jasper that he would never see himself at that age, but he refused to let it get in the way of his happy reunion with his friend. He buried the dark thought and silenced the voice.

He poured Oliver a drink and listened to stories of his travels, and how successful his foreign investments were. Jasper was proud of his friend, and at that moment, he recalled that Oliver controlled a large portion of the Clifford Coal Factory. Perhaps he would save the dying business, now that he was back with enough experience and wealth.

An even better notion would be Jasper inquiring about it and investing. He wanted to help Natalie's family in the most respectable manner possible, and he will. Heavens knows the Earl deserved the help, too. Now, however, was not the time to broach the topic.

"You have returned in time for a soirée Aunt Phoebe is hosting."

"Oh, is it in honor of my return?" Oliver asked, raising a blonde brow.

That gave Jasper the idea, and he decided to host it in honor of his friend. Oliver had practically been raised in Amsthorne Manor, and they were more brothers than friends. They had done everything from causing mischief in Eton to roaming the streets of London, wild with youth and vigor. He deserved to have the soirée hosted in his honor.

"Wait here," Jasper said with a grin. "I will fetch Aunt Phoebe."

He hurried out of the room and found her leaving the music room. Taking her hand, he said, "Oliver has returned."

"Oh, goodness! That is marvelous news!"

They entered the study, and Phoebe was truly delighted to see Oliver again. and vice versa. She even went on to suggest he marry, now that he had returned to England and that there were many young ladies to choose from.

Jasper shook his head, muttering, "Why does this not surprise me?"

"If you are too exhausted from your travels to seek, you may appoint me as your matchmaker," she offered, and Oliver roared with laughter.

He glanced at Jasper. "Our dear Phoebe has not changed."

"She never will, Oliver," Jasper chuckled.

"Lord knows you need a wife, especially now that you are an earl," Phoebe added, pinning them both with that maternal look of admonishment.

"Lady Phoebe, I have only just returned," Oliver protested with a fond smile.

"That is why I offered to help, Oliver," she responded.

"And this is what I contend with every day," Jasper said, and his aunt glared at him before joining in their mirth.

"Although, I have no qualms about getting married now," Oliver suddenly announced.

"Finally," Phoebe threw her hands in the air in a theatrical show of relief.

"If you would do me the honor of being my bride, Lady Phoebe," Oliver added impishly.

"You scoundrel!" Phoebe swatted his shoulder, and they laughed more at the ridiculous joke.

"Aunt Phoebe," Jasper claimed her attention, "why don't we host the soiree in Oliver's honor to celebrate his return to England? What say you?"

Phoebe clapped her hands together. "Certainly! I would be delighted to." Oliver tried to decline courteously, but she refused to listen. Jasper did not have to insist, for his aunt was very convincing. "You should know me after all our years together, Oliver. I never accept negative answers." She left Oliver no choice but to agree.

Chapter Twenty

A pair of masks that could only belong to the Rogue and the Comtesse was found on a ship that was to sail to the East Indies tomorrow. The sailor who found it was an ardent reader of The Londoner, and one could only imagine his joy when he brought the masks to us. Before the day ended, however, several pairs of masks were discovered aboard ships. Now, what manner of devilry is this? Misleading an entire town is unforgivable.

Tonight, Natalie took great pains in her toilette, and as she raised her hands to pinch her cheeks on her way downstairs, she realized she did not have to do that. She needed only to think about Jasper for the heat to put color on her face. No matter what she told herself, she had to admit that she was trying to look her best for Jasper.

Hannah also looked marvelous in a pale blue dress that complimented her dark hair and pale skin. They left for the soirée shortly, and an hour later, they arrived at Amsthorne Manor.

In the ballroom, she looked around for Jasper, but he was nowhere in sight, and something uneasy settled within her. Phoebe, however, was very much present, and she greeted them joyfully, introducing George to the Earl of Liverpool, who happened to be the Prime Minister.

Such an acquaintance could never be a waste, and George looked truly hopeful for the first time in a long while. Perhaps their luck was finally changing.

As they stood with Phoebe and several guests, Natalie spied a tall figure that could be Jasper, but when the gentleman turned, disappointment washed over her despite her efforts to keep it at bay. She had put forth so much effort for him to see her tonight, and it would be a shame if he was not present.

Wessberg came to claim a dance with Hannah while Phoebe's attention was taken by a countess with a boisterous laugh. Natalie was left to decorate the fringes of the ballroom as she was accustomed to doing, yet it felt different and even more humiliating tonight.

To her surprise, a young man approached her, introducing himself as the Marquess Hillward. He looked like he was no older than twenty, but for the purpose of being polite, Natalie returned his greeting in kind.

"May I have a dance, My Lady?" He held out his arm, and her eyes fleetingly moved across the room to seek an excuse to decline. Finding none, she stifled a sigh and accepted with a smile.

The dance was, thankfully, a quadrille. They did not converse, and their steps were quick. Natalie's eyes continued to move dolefully across the ballroom in search of Jasper, even though she knew she would not find him.

After the dance, the Marquess bowed politely. "Thank you for the honor, My Lady." He offered her his arm again, and they took a silent turn about the room before they stopped by the refreshment table.

He picked up a glass of champagne and was handing it to her when he caught sight of something behind her, and his hand shook slightly. Curious, Natalie turned to find Jasper smiling down at her.

Something lit within her, and her rigid shoulders relaxed. His gaze traveled slowly over her, and Natalie felt as though he was disrobing her. Her lips parted as she grew breathless. She absently registered the Marquess leaving them, but her attention was on Jasper and how handsome he looked in his black evening attire.

"I thought you were not coming," she said, and his eyes flared with desire before he took her hand and raised it to his lips.

"I could never pass the chance to see you, Natalie." As his lips touched her gloved hand, warmth seeped into her that made her eyelids heavy, and her heart beat faster. "Something required my attention and caused me to be late. I hope I did not keep you waiting for too long."

"I suffered a dance with the Marquess of Hillward."

Jasper winced. "Forgive me, darling." The word rolled from his lips like silk and wrapped around her possessively. She loved it.

"Very well." She accepted the champagne he offered her and took a sip, something giddy forming inside her.

"Is there a wish you want to strike off tonight?" Jasper asked her almost conspiratorially.

Natalie thought before saying, "I want to ask a gentleman to dance."

Jasper straightened and grinned. "Go on, then."

Her eyes narrowed briefly before she turned and began to search the room. "Are you looking for something?" he asked when she did not answer.

"Some*one*," she corrected.

"I think the person you seek is standing right before you, Natalie." Jasper took her arm and turned her to face him. Her brows creased momentarily before she realized what he was referring to.

"You want me to ask *you* to dance?" She smiled up at him.

"Who else would you ask? " he returned.

"I cannot ask you because it would be too easy to complete the task. I want to ask a gentleman who could think me mad." The entire challenge was to ask a stranger, someone who could deny her. Jasper would do no such thing.

"Very well, then," he said, and she was rather surprised that he acquiesced so easily. Natalie thought he would argue with her.

His keen blue gaze swept the ballroom before he suddenly pointed to a gentleman who had his back to them and said, "You may ask that gentleman." There was a dare in his tone, and Natalie all but confidently accepted the challenge.

That confidence was only pronounced in his presence, however, for when she started walking toward the gentleman, she felt her legs weaken and her heart race. The man was conversing with an elderly lord and still had his back to her. The older lord's gaze landed on her when she approached.

"My lord," Natalie said as she curtsied gracefully before shifting her attention onto the younger gentlemen, who she was about to ask to dance.

When he turned to look down at her, the blood swiftly drained from her face, as the breath left her. *Oliver Bargrave?* she almost blurted out, but shock seemed to have robbed her of speech.

Oliver looked just as surprised as she felt, and upon noticing the shift in his demeanor, Natalie quickly gathered her wits. The elderly lord's attention was fortunately sought by someone else right then, and she saw an opportunity. She could not balk after finding that it was her nemesis, and she could feel Jasper's eyes on her.

"My Lord," she said stiffly, curtsying.

He bowed. "How good to see you, Lady Natalie. I truly did not expect to find you at this ball."

Liar! "Of course," she murmured. "May I ask you to dance with me?"

Oliver's gray eyes widened, and his blonde eyebrows that matched his hair ascended. "I...why, yes. Yes, you may dance with me." His fluster gave her some satisfaction, and as she accepted his proffered arm and allowed him to lead her to the dance floor, she glanced behind to see Jasper smiling proudly at her. Did he truly have no inkling of what was happening, or had he purposefully chosen Oliver to test her?

He had no recollection of the events of that night a decade ago. Or did he?

"I must declare that you gave me quite the shock tonight, Lady Natalie," Oliver's smug voice tore into her thoughts, and something bitter rose in her throat. He was a handsome man, but his cruelty had divested him of any good qualities in her eyes. Oliver was the most contemptible person she had ever had the misfortune of knowing.

He appeared utterly unbothered by her glare. Surely, he was still very much aware of his crimes, was he not? His life was probably better for those. He was a man with no conscience at all. "An old friend asking another to dance after a while?" she asked. "Where is the shock in that, Lord Bargrave?" Natalie gave a confident tilt of her head as the dance began.

The gesture drew Oliver's attention to her person now, and he allowed his gaze the liberty of assessing her before a lascivious gleam took over his eyes. Natalie felt a shudder of disgust run through her.

"You are looking fine, Lady Natalie," he observed. "I must say that the years seem to have favored more than just your appearance, for I would never have thought to see the day Lady Natalie Reeves would walk up to me and ask me to dance. I declare myself honored," he finished.

Natalie ground her teeth. She had no confidence or any sense of her worth before he left England, and he was quick to remind her of where she had been and belittle her for it. They changed partners, and this gave her a chance to regain her composure.

"Time brings with it change, My Lord," she answered calmly when they met again, "and with change comes growth."

"Quite so," Oliver murmured, his eyes moving over her body again.

"Well, for most of us, at least," she added with a deliberate smile. He had neither changed nor matured, after all these years, for only an immature person would seek to undermine others.

Oliver flushed with irritation at her subtle insult, but he tried to conceal it. Nonetheless, Natalie allowed herself all the satisfaction she could feel.

Oliver made a quick recovery. "Some things remain unchanged with you, Lady Natalie."

Natalie gave an indifferent shrug despite her internal turmoil. "So long as I am comfortable with those things, it should not matter."

The dance ended, much to her relief, but he was greatly displeased. "We shall meet again," he said to her as she curtsied, and he bowed. Natalie could not help but feel as though he had just promised her future retribution with his words to meet again.

She sought an excuse to leave the soiree early, and she went so far as to pretend she was poorly. Oliver's words had greatly unsettled her, and his reappearance had opened a wound she thought was healing.

When she saw Jasper approach her, she turned and found the first exit. She simply could not believe that he had not intentionally chosen Oliver to dance with her.

The following afternoon, Oliver made an unexpected call upon their house, and he spent quite some time with George in his study.

Natalie paced the drawing room, knots in her stomach. Unable to bear the thought of disrupting a good night for her cousins, she had hired a hack and left the soirée, leaving a note for Phoebe and expressing her regrets.

Of course, she had continued to pretend to be unwell throughout the morning until afternoon came and Oliver visited. At last, Oliver and George entered the drawing room, and a disgustingly smug smile spread across his lips.

"It appears as though we would be seeing more of each other now, Natalie," he said to her before glancing in a displeased George's direction and giving him a deliberate smile. She also noted that he called her by her Christian name. Once more, his words hung over her like a dark cloud.

After his departure, Natalie raised her eyes to George's, and he looked grim and older than his years. "What did he want?" Oliver had to have demanded the impossible. It was his way.

George shook his head. "It is just business. Only the coal factory. Nothing more." He turned and walked back to his study, leaving Natalie confused and pained.

Hannah was out with her friend, and Natalie distracted herself with her sewing until evening came. George did not join her and Hannah for dinner, and that was when Natalie knew that something was gravely wrong.

After their meal, she decided to find him in his study. When she knocked, he called, "I am busy. Come back later."

"I need to speak to you, George," she said.

After several seconds, he called for her to enter. She walked in to find him drinking by the hearth. He did not turn to look at her, but she somehow saw the shadows in his eyes.

Moving close, she placed a hand on his shoulder. "What did Oliver want, George?"

"Uncle Hubert gave him the house, Natalie."

Darkness descended over her, graying her vision. Her hand moved from his shoulder to clutch the back of his chair to keep herself steady. "What did you say?"

"This house now belongs to Oliver. Uncle Hubert gave it to him when he asked for it." He drank the remainder of the liquor in his glass while Natalie thought she would faint.

"No," she shook her head. "It cannot be. Father could not have done that."

"He came with proof, Natalie. It was complete with the late Earl's signature. Our beloved townhouse belongs to Ecklehill." George sounded as heartbroken as she felt.

The townhouse was all they had left, and now it appeared as though it was no longer theirs. They could not sell it to better their lives, no matter how desperate they were.

"Oliver says that we can keep the house," George carried on, and she straightened to listen, "in exchange for Hannah's hand in marriage." Her eyes grew wide as she took a step back. This pained her more than if a blow had been dealt to her gut. "We cannot let Hannah find out, Natalie," George said.

Natalie turned toward the door and saw Hannah standing in the doorway. "She already knows," she whispered.

"Are you still keeping things from me?" Hannah asked as she walked into the room. "I thought we understood each other better now."

Natalie felt it was wrong to keep it from her, as she had every right to know about the demand being made. "We are not keeping anything from you."

"That is not what I heard George say just now."

Natalie gave her cousin the news, her heart aching when she saw the color drain from Hannah's face. Tears quickly brimmed her eyes, and she caught her bottom lip between her teeth.

"What if he truly takes the house away from us?" Hannah asked.

"Do not think about it," Natalie quickly said when she gathered the direction Hannah's thoughts were headed. "*Nothing* is worth giving up your happiness for, Hannah. Do you hear me? *Nothing!*"

"Not even family?" Hannah asked, and Natalie found herself unable to answer that question. "Good night," Hannah said when she did not respond and stalked out of the room.

Natalie wanted to follow her and comfort her, but she decided to allow some time for the news to settle. They were all shocked, and poor George seemed to have taken the matter worse than all of them.

Chapter Twenty-One

Lord Rogue and his Comtesse have disappeared after tricking all of us. And have we mentioned that the Comtesse won more than two thousand pounds from Mr. Lupton and Baron Phelps? Her skill should be admired, but not when men are losing to her. It is shameful.

The following afternoon, Natalie had just returned from a trip to Mary's shop when she met the family physician waiting for her in the drawing room. Her stomach turned, and worry gripped her when she entered and saw Dr. Rivers.

She wondered who he was here for, as Hannah had been anything but herself when Natalie checked on her earlier that morning. Understandably so, too.

"Lady Natalie," he greeted.

"Are you here for George?" she asked, and his expression turned more serious.

"Yes, My Lady. I fear His Lordship is not doing better." Natalie inhaled and tried to keep her composure. She held the back of the chair she was standing by. "I fear that not even his young age can carry on working in his favor."

"What exactly is the matter with him?" she asked. "Please do not keep it from me."

"It is his heart, My Lady. His heart is unwell. I thought I should inform you despite promising that I would not say a word about it to you."

"Thank you for telling me, Dr. Rivers."

Upon his departure, she slumped into one of the chairs, contemplating what they had done wrong to deserve the blows life was constantly dealing them.

"Was that the doctor?" Hannah's voice came from the door. Natalie sat up, relieved to see her out of her room at last. "It is George again, is it not?" Natalie nodded, and her cousin came to sit in the chair opposite her. "We may have a solution to all of these problems in our hands, you know."

"No, Hannah," Natalie argued. She could not allow her cousin to sacrifice herself. "We are not selling you to Oliver," she ground out.

"Then, for how long will we carry on living like this? There is only so long George can hold on. And are you going to continue sewing for the rest of your life? Something must be done, Natalie. Oliver just offered us a way out of misery." Hannah was tearing up, and Natalie went to her, wrapping her arms around her trembling shoulders.

"What about Wessberg, Hannah?" Natalie smoothed her dark hair. "You love him, do you not?" More tears streamed down Hannah's cheeks at the mention of Wessberg, and Natalie got her answer.

"I love *you*, Natalie, and George, too," she protested. "You are the only family I know."

"George and I shall do whatever it will take to give you your happiness," Natalie vowed, pulling her into a hug and encouraging her to cry as much as she needed to.

When Hannah was calm, she went to brew some tea in the kitchen with Cook's help, and Natalie decided to write a letter. After sealing it, she gave it to the butler and asked him to have it delivered to Oliver immediately. She needed to meet with him privately. In the letter, she had chosen a meeting place and time. She was not young and stupid anymore as to leave such things to him now.

Three hours after sending the letter, Oliver sent a response, agreeing to meet her. She left the house shortly and found the small tea shop she had chosen.

Natalie was shown to a table in a corner, and she sat to wait for him, anger warring with her nerves. A half-hour later, Oliver appeared. He had made her wait for him, and his expression all but revealed his pleasure.

"To what do I owe the pleasure of such urgent summons, Natalie?" he derided as he sat across from her. It was a respectable tea shop, and she was glad that everyone there was not paying them any attention.

"What do you want from my family?" she asked without responding to his nonsense. "What pleasure do you find in tormenting us?"

He turned and summoned a waiter. When the man appeared, he ordered tea for them. Then he leaned back in his seat and watched her as though she had not just asked him a question.

Nevertheless, she continued. "Have you not taken enough already, Oliver?" she asked, desperately trying to contain her ire and bitterness.

"Oh, but I never took anything, Natalie," he responded at length. "Everything I got, I earned. Through *your* carelessness."

"And you are proud of it?" Natalie whispered, horrified. She held her breath to deal with the fact that he had just blamed her for her family's misery.

"On the contrary, I am simply stating the truth," he smirked.

"Hannah will not marry you," Natalie said matter-of-factly.

"It is not your decision to make," he shot back.

Natalie had never felt more hopeless in her life, but she maintained her stance. "You will keep away from my family. What you took from us is enough." If they were to emerge defeated after everything, then she wanted them to walk away with their pride and dignity, at least.

"I see you wish to be homeless."

"You are not my maker or the keeper of my fate. We will keep our house, and Hannah will not marry you."

"You are making a grave mistake." He shot to his feet. "Do not allow your foolishness to birth another disaster in your life." He turned without allowing her to say anything more and walked out of the shop, leaving her fighting an internal war she was no longer sure she could win.

The waiter brought the tea, and she told him that the man who ordered it had left, then she took her leave, too.

Dejected, she returned home, and when she walked into the front hall, she met the butler bearing a tea tray for George. "I will take it to him," she mumbled, collecting the tray.

He was in his study, a deep frown on his face and his bespectacled eyes moving over lines of correspondence. He was still occupied despite the physician's visit.

George looked up, and he was surprised to see her bearing the tea. "I thought you would be abed after Dr. Rivers' visit."

He winced. "Did the butler tell you about it?"

She poured some tea into a cup for him and placed some biscuits onto a smaller plate, taking them to him. Then she sat before the desk and regarded him.

"Whatever it is, say it." George took a sip of his tea. "What could possibly be worse than the recent events?"

"I spoke to Dr. Rivers myself," Natalie announced. "He told me everything."

George let out a curse under his breath. "I warned him not to—"

"Why, George?" Natalie interrupted. "If he does not tell us, *your* family, who should he share it with? Who should give you the support you need?"

"I should be the one giving you and Hannah support," George said miserably. "But every day, I am failing to bear that responsibility. Look at you, Natalie. You were raised with every luxury afforded to man, but you now live toiling like a commoner. My heart breaks every time I see light streaming from underneath your bedchamber door because I know you are by the candle sewing."

Natalie knew his fears without him telling her, and she wished, more than anything, that she could change his feelings of inadequacy.

She countered what he said, and she reassured him. "We will get through this, George." Natalie reached for his hand across the table and held it tightly. "We can weather this if we stay strong *together*."

There had to be another way to defeat Oliver. She had been trying not to think of Jasper, but he continued to come into her thoughts.

Chapter Twenty-Two

Lady Phoebe Dawson's soiree was resplendent, but we were disappointed before it ended. Lady Natalie Reeves, the newly crowned darling of the beau monde, fled the event. Why? If you have the answer, please come forward and aid us in solving another mystery that has descended upon us.

"You know, I think I just might heed Lady Phoebe's advice," Oliver declared.

Jasper quirked an inquisitive brow. He had called upon Oliver, and they were playing billiards in his game room. Jasper was playing to distract himself. Natalie had left the soirée without her family, and he wanted to know why.

He could write to her, but he wanted her to tell him whatever it was in person. He had been conversing with another gentleman while she danced with Oliver, thus, he did not know what happened after the dance that chased her away.

"I am considering marriage," Oliver elaborated.

A smile touched Jasper's features. "I never thought I would live to see the day Oliver Bargrave would consider getting leg-shackled. What changed your mind? And who is the fortunate lady?"

"I have not decided, but Clifford's sister seems delightful." Oliver took his turn while Jasper's body tensed.

"Lady Natalie?" he asked, wondering if he had shot himself in the knee by suggesting Oliver to Natalie as a dance partner. Could it be that after just that one encounter, Oliver fancied her now? Was he the reason she ran away?

"Oh, as interesting as Lady Natalie is, I am afraid she is not my choice. I speak of Miss Hannah Reeves," Oliver replied. Jasper felt himself go weak with relief.

"Good." He cleared his throat after realizing what he had just said. "That is to say, Miss Reeves is a good young lady."

Oliver chuckled. "You are flustered by the news of my intention to seek a wife. Something the matter?"

"Not at all." The thought of Natalie with another man corroded his mind. He played a turn after Oliver, and then he thought of something. He decided to invite the family to the manor for dinner. After all, it would give him a reason to speak to Natalie and learn why she left.

Since Oliver and Clifford were good business partners, it would be a good opportunity for Jasper to learn about the business and for his friend to spend time with Miss Reeves.

Jasper told him his plan, and something odd passed over Oliver's features before he declared that it was a good idea. They continued their game, and Oliver began to inquire about what Jasper had done while he was away.

"Don't say that you have not met anyone of interest, Jasper," Oliver remarked impishly, and the image of Natalie writhing in his arms invaded Jasper's thoughts.

"Oh, with that sort of expression on your face, I think there definitely is someone you are hiding," Oliver chuckled.

Jasper dismissed his friend's suspicions, but deep within him, he found a part of him thinking about Natalie and how he wished they could mean more to each other. He tried, with some success, to return his attention to the game, but his lungs were being starved of air again.

"Your dream is coming true, Aunt Phoebe," Jasper said as he walked into the drawing room that evening. "Oliver has found a lady he wants to marry."

"Truly?" Phoebe set down her book and sat up.

"Yes. He finds Miss Hannah Reeves, in his words, *delightful*," he continued. "As a matter of fact, he intends to offer for her. I told him that I would host the family for dinner."

His aunt smiled. "Our numbers are even then. While Oliver keeps Miss Reeves company, you shall be with Lady Natalie." Jasper thought her choice of words, 'be with Lady Natalie,' was deliberate, but he said nothing. "Don't you think this is a sign, Jasper?" Phoebe asked.

"What sign, Auntie?"

"A sign for you from your friend to select your bride, too," she replied.

"Not again, Auntie. We have talked about this," Jasper sighed.

Phoebe ignored his protest and carried on. "Oliver recently returned to the country, and he is already thinking of marriage. Why can you not do the same after all these years?"

"Oliver is not dying anytime soon!" Jasper snapped before he could control his emotions. "He will not leave his wife widowed shortly after marriage. He will not be placed in the ground filled with regret about dashing a young woman's dreams. And God forbid he leave her with child."

His aunt's eyes widened, and she raised a hand to her chest. "Oh, come now, Jasper, do not tell me that you still dwell on that and believe those baseless superstitions." Phoebe's regard was nervous, and there was a tremor in her voice.

"Let us be realistic for once, auntie. Do you think it mere coincidence that both father and grandfather died at the same age and of mysterious illnesses? What are the odds of such happening in a family?" He waited patiently for her answer. Her features wrinkled with something akin to worry.

"*Nothing* is going to happen to you, Jasper." Phoebe rose and wrapped her arms around him. "I will not allow anything to happen to you, my child." It sounded to Jasper as though she was somehow trying to convince herself now.

"Father and grandfather had strange headaches, and within hours, they died." He pulled away and held her shoulders. For the first time, it appeared Phoebe was beginning to truly consider his condition. She looked afraid. "Both shortly after their thirty-fifth year."

"I will not allow it." She shook her head.

"You cannot do anything, auntie," Jasper said. He did not want her giving him hope or harboring any hope herself. They would both certainly be disappointed, and that was not the way he wanted to leave her. It was always best to keep one's heart protected. Tears streamed down her cheeks, and he drew her close.

"I would die before I let go of you, Jasper," she vowed, sniffling against his chest. He blinked against the emotion blurring his vision.

That night, the Rogue traveled to East End, but he did not gamble. He found a pub and sat at a table, drinking and pondering his life; the people in it he did not want to lose or bid farewell.

Natalie continued to sit at the fore of those thoughts, and Jasper let out a snort at how ridiculous everything was. Natalie may desire him, but he meant no more than that to her.

Chapter Twenty-Three

Miss Alexandra Gilmore appears to know why Lady Natalie Reeves left the soiree early. Our dear Miss Gilmore should know that we do not hide names in The Londoner. As we have yet to receive more news about the Masked Rogue, we shall have to make London wait until tomorrow to read what we learned from Miss Gilmore.

Hannah found Natalie doing some sewing in the conservatory. She had wanted a change of scenery to clear her head further and had elected to sit in this room.

"Have you noticed how awfully quiet the Masked Rogue has become lately?" Her cousin pursed her lips in contemplation. "Do you think he has left us to live in France with his Comtesse? I don't have anything to write with him gone."

"He is quiet, Hannah," Natalie responded, rummaging through the basket of sewing items. "And I do not think he is in France."

"You sound certain."

"I do not know," Natalie sighed.

"It is utterly unlike him to go days without causing mischief about town," Hannah insisted.

"Perhaps he is being careful these days because of excessively inquisitive writers like you," Natalie mentioned.

"George is not helping matters either," Hannah slumped petulantly into a nearby chair.

"George?" Natalie looked up. "What business has George got to do with the Masked Rogue or your articles?"

"He is refusing to take the suggestion and challenge the Masked Rogue after his victory against Amsthorne," Hannah grumbled. "If only brother would agree to the game, I could use him to find out the Rogue's identity." Hannah looked askance at Natalie as she said that, and she was sure the question was deliberate. She did not want George to help her find the Rogue because she already knew.

George was too bothered to think of anything else, and Natalie was certain a game with the Rogue was the last thing on his mind. She wanted to tell her that George's heart was ill because of their problems, but she was afraid. Returning to Hannah's argument, George had already played and won against the Rogue, Natalie thought with a little smile.

"What is that smile on your face, Natalie?" Hannah moved to the edge of her seat and squinted.

"I hope you are not in want of spectacles, too," Natalie teased.

"Certainly not!"

"Then can I not smile without it being suspect simply because you're starved of news of the Rogue, Hannah?" Natalie found the thimble she was looking for and stared momentarily at her calloused fingers. They used to be very soft, and she longed to have them back in that state.

"I *am* starved!" Hannah gave a melodramatic cry just as the butler walked in, bearing an invitation. She ran to him. "Who is it from this time?"

They were all trying to convince themselves that nothing in their life had changed after Oliver's offer, but they could deny it today and tomorrow, but not for too long.

"Another invitation from Amsthorne?" Hannah asked as she opened the invitation. "Oh, dinner with just our family!" She laughed, and her eyes gleamed. "I told you that the Duke fancies you, Natalie. Why else would he send a dinner invitation? Such an intimate one, too?"

Natalie's stomach clenched.

"I think it is from Phoebe. She is our good friend, and naturally, she would invite us to dinner. Do you know how far the manor is from the city and how lonely she could become?" Natalie made all of these points to tell herself that the invitation was not from Jasper. She longed to see him again, but she was also conflicted about him and his place in Oliver's twisted schemes. Especially after the dance.

Color slowly crept to her neck and face, and she looked away from Hannah before she began to suspect anything. Could it truly be? That warmth reached her heart at the thought of Jasper wanting her beyond his desire.

"And you are fond of him, too!" Hannah exclaimed the instant she caught the color on her face.

"Do not be silly, Hannah!" Natalie dismissed.

"That sounds like you saying, *do not tell me the truth, Hannah*," her cousin giggled impishly.

Natalie laughed, and every part of her fluttered. She allowed herself to push her doubts about Jasper away. He had been kind to her, and she had changed her mind about revenge. Her enemy now was Oliver.

TESSA BROOKMAN

Every excited shiver or knot of anticipation Natalie felt vanished the instant they were shown into the manor's drawing room, and she saw Oliver seated at the pianoforte, playing.

"Oh, you have arrived!" A delighted Phoebe approached them, and Natalie was forced to smile. George stood rigidly beside her while Hannah's face grew pale.

Thankfully, Phoebe did not notice, and she turned to Oliver as she walked to where they stood, an assured smile now on his face.

"I do not believe I have had the opportunity to introduce the Earl of Ecklehill," she said just as Jasper appeared.

Natalie tried to look indifferent as Oliver greeted them, but as soon as Jasper took her hand, a strange calmness washed over her. It was as though his very presence was countering every menacing look Oliver surreptitiously cast in her direction.

He kissed her hand. "I am happy to see you this evening, My Lady."

Phoebe and George looked pleased, but when Oliver spoke to Hannah, George's demeanor changed to one of dire consternation.

Dinner was announced, saving them from talking longer in the drawing room. There would be conversation while they ate, but they could distract themselves with the food. Oliver walked with Hannah, unfortunately, while George accompanied Phoebe.

When Jasper took Natalie's hand again, she could not help the little flutter she felt at the contact. He grinned slyly as he placed her hand on his elbow and led her to the dining room.

Conversation at dinner was unsurprisingly dominated by Oliver as he shared stories of his travels and business adventures. He boasted at every opportunity, and although Phoebe and Jasper were unaware of it —likely because he was their good friend and their judgment was shaded—Natalie's family was losing their spirits.

She looked up from her soup and found Jasper's eyes on her. His expression was unreadable, but Natalie thought she saw a hint of displeasure in his eyes.

Then George surprised her when he began to participate in the conversation with more spirit. He asked Oliver questions, and Oliver replied pleasantly. *The vile demon!* She smiled when she heard the sarcasm in her cousin's compliments, which Oliver was oblivious to.

Phoebe conversed with Hannah, and Jasper claimed Natalie's attention. "You are quiet tonight. Is something the matter?"

Natalie smiled at him and shook her head. "Cook is very skilled with partridge. I am afraid that is what has me quiet tonight."

He laughed softly, but she could see that he did not believe her. He did not prod her, and she appreciated it along with his concern. Dinner passed better than she thought, and when it was over, the ladies left the gentlemen to enjoy their port, moving to the drawing room.

Phoebe played the pianoforte while Hannah sang, and Natalie's mood was rejuvenated. That was until Oliver entered the room and sidled beside her. Hannah missed a note when she saw him, but Phoebe continued playing, encouraging her to keep singing.

"I told you we would be seeing each other more frequently, Natalie," Oliver said.

"You left your company to tell me this?" she asked, quirking an eyebrow.

"I came to tell you something different, my dear—"

"Do not call me that!" she whispered harshly.

Oliver ignored her and continued. "Do you not find it curious that Amsthorne bears no recollection of that night?" Natalie gave no response to this as something constricted her chest. "We tend to erase our most insignificant memories, after all. I suppose he is excused in that regard," Oliver chuckled.

Natalie felt her nails dig painfully into her palms. Oliver might not stop until he had her family's blood.

"Would you like some water, Natalie? You look rather parched." He feigned concern. He knew the pain he was causing her, and he was thoroughly enjoying it.

"Please, excuse me." Natalie rose stiffly. She might perish if she spent another minute in his vile company.

She found the lavatory and patted some cold water onto her face. It was soothing, but it did little in the way of calming the emotions that warred inside her. Anger took her breath away while sadness pushed against the back of her eyes. She regarded herself in the mirror, seeing how disturbed she looked.

Slowly, and with considerable effort, she forced a smile onto her face. When she was satisfied, she let herself out of the room. As she opened the door and stepped into the hallway, she let out a small gasp.

"Did I frighten you?" Jasper asked, pushing off the wall he had been leaning against, waiting for her. His eyes narrowed, and his brows furrowed. "Are you well?" Before she could respond, he took her hand and drew her into the first room he found, locking it behind them.

"There is no reason to lock us in here, Jasper," she laughed nervously. "I am well."

His skeptical gaze remained on her, searching every inch of her face to confirm what she had just said.

"I do not believe you. You left the soiree abruptly, you were too quiet at dinner, and now you look as though you are going to cry." Jasper took her face in his hands. "Natalie, my darling, tell me what troubles you."

The softness of his tone and the concern in his eyes made her truly wish that she could cry and tell him what bothered her, but he was a part of those things.

"Natalie?" he asked again, bringing his lips very close to hers. Instead of answering, she met him the rest of the way, and the passion that had been swelling erupted between them.

She wrapped her arms around his neck and pressed herself against him, while his mouth moved over hers with both sweetness and urgency. He guided her to a table and placed her atop it, his hands caressing her body through her dress, reminding her of the never-ending need she had, and that only he could satisfy.

Jasper kissed her neck, his hands bunching her skirts up and reaching underneath to caress her thighs. As she raked her hands through his hair with her eyes closed, he slipped off her shoe and rolled one of her stockings down her leg, taking it off. "I will keep this," he murmured, smiling wickedly at her.

At that instant, Natalie pushed away everything she held against him. He knew how to please her, and that was what she needed to escape her troubles for a short while. "What else will you keep?" she asked slyly, giving him a look that dared him.

"My name on your lips." It sounded like a vow, and Natalie understood his meaning when he pushed her skirts further up and reached between her legs.

Chapter Twenty-Four

Miss Alexandra Gilmore revealed to The Londoner that the Duke of Amsthorne told Lady Natalie Reeves that he had no wish to make her his duchess. A broken heart? No, that cannot be the reason Lady Natalie left Lady Phoebe Dawson's soirée. It is true that the Duke might never marry, but it pains us to learn that our dear Lady Natalie might be heartbroken. Is there any truth in this tale? Surely, we should not disbelieve the word of the good Miss Gilmore, should we?

"Jasper," Natalie moaned, her pleasure swelling everywhere he touched her.

"Open your eyes, darling," he instructed, touching his lips to hers. "I want to see those lovely eyes while I give you pleasure."

She opened them, and his intense blue gaze held her, stealing her breath away. He stroked her moist center, and her eyelids fluttered. Her blood burned, and the more he stroked her, the more she wanted.

Natalie took hold of his coat lapels, leaning back against the wall on the other side of the table. Jasper lifted one of her legs and held it, slipping his fingers into her. She breathed his name, and his lips spread into the most devilish grin she had ever seen him wear.

His strokes grew frantic, and their gaze remained locked, intensifying every ounce of pleasure that he was giving her. Natalie's heart beat faster, and her nerves coiled and tightened luxuriously until she trembled, unable to breathe. His eyes seemed to look into her soul, and she wanted to look away, but like a woman trapped under a spell, she remained.

Her fingers tightened around his coat lapels until her knuckles were white, and Natalie clenched her teeth to keep from crying out as an exquisitely gratifying wave overtook her, scattering her senses. Jasper withdrew his hand from her center and wrapped his arms around her waist, holding her tightly against him.

"Natalie, darling," he whispered in her ear while he ran his hand up and down her back. She clung to him as her body calmed and that beautiful and familiar warmth covered her. He pulled back and looked down at her. "Did I keep my promise?"

"Is that a serious question?" she chuckled. He had done more than simply keep a promise because what he had done to her tonight would remain in her memories for a very long time—if it would ever leave.

"It is a serious question, Natalie." He took her face between his hands. "Your satisfaction is important to me." His gaze had softened, and she thought he was no longer asking about the pleasure he had just given her.

"You did," she answered, and he smiled. His lips parted as though he was going to say more to her but he only kissed her.

When he pulled away, she still thought he would speak, but he did not. Jasper pulled her skirts down and straightened the neckline of her dress before helping her smoothen her hair. Then he helped her off the table and led her to a mirror near the door. He stood behind her and kissed her shoulder.

Natalie's body was still singing, but as she regarded their reflection, her senses floated more toward desire. She saw the question in his eyes, and he was asking her if her appearance was good enough for her to return to the drawing room without rousing anyone's suspicions. Natalie nodded.

Smiling, Jasper turned her around and unlocked the door. "I will join you momentarily." His hands remained on her shoulders, and she found herself reluctant to part with him, too. "What is your next wish?" he asked.

A smile curved her lips. "I want to fence."

His brows rose ever so slightly, but he did not remark upon it and only said, "It shall be arranged."

Natalie opened the door and left. It was not difficult to find her way back to the drawing room, and she paused by the door, both to catch her breath and to fortify her nerves before she saw Oliver.

He was not in the room when she entered, however, and Hannah and George looked freer. Then Phoebe informed her that he had departed early to handle some business. The tension in her shoulders eased, and she went to sit near Hannah.

Natalie knew her relief was momentary because Oliver was back in England, and he would not stop tormenting her so quickly.

⋆⋆⋆

GEORGE FOLDED THE NEWSPAPER AND SHOOK HIS HEAD, INCITING Natalie to incline her head and study him.

"What does the news say?" she asked.

"Only foolish predictions. The person who wrote the news I finished reading thinks Oliver will revive the Clifford Coal Factory and Mines."

"Did Oliver tell them that?" Hannah asked, scowling.

"He could have," George responded. "Did you hear him talk about his accomplishments last night?" It was evident how wounded her cousin was by Oliver's boasts.

Natalie sighed and bit into her toast. She did not particularly wish to discuss Oliver this morning, but George was allowed to vent, and she understood how frustrated he was.

"I cannot believe that someone as good as Amsthorne would keep the company of such a man," he continued. "Is the Duke aware of his treacherous nature?"

"I doubt he is," Natalie said. She had thought about this before and assumed Jasper was as corrupt as Oliver was, but as she learned of the manner of man Jasper was, she found her opinion changing.

She could not tell whether she had forgiven Jasper for what he had done to her, but her regard for him had softened. He was in her thoughts nearly every moment of the day, and he had awakened her body to desires she never imagined herself capable of feeling. And then there was her heart, which she was desperately trying to shield from him.

"I agree," George said. "I will not believe he would associate with him knowing that."

Natalie wondered if her cousins would hold the same opinion if they knew of the role Jasper had played ten years ago, but then she recalled how gentle and caring he had been the night before. *He is a good man. He has to be.*

The thoughts were disquieting, and after breakfast, Natalie decided to do some sewing in her bedchamber. Hannah followed her, however, and she looked as though she had a hundred questions to ask Natalie.

"You seemed quite distracted at breakfast," Hannah began, sitting on the bed and watching Natalie gather her sewing items and sit by the window. "Is everything well?"

"No," Natalie sighed. "Everything is not well because of Oliver."

"My question does not relate to Oliver," Hannah corrected, and some color crept onto Natalie's cheeks.

"I do not know what you are asking, then." It was better to pretend she did not know than to tell her cousin that she was confused by her feelings.

"The Duke, Natalie," Hannah grinned. "I am asking about him."

She did not know what to tell her, and to quiet Hannah, she said. "We are going to fence."

Her cousin's eyes rounded. "That is on your list?"

"Yes. I want to learn to fence, then play against a gentleman." Natalie knew how to fence but she had forgotten some things because it had been very long since she last picked up a foil.

Hannah grew excited. She bounced on the bed, and her eyes gleamed as she asked several more questions. "What will you wear? Something seductive?"

"To fence in?" Natalie laughed.

"No, before that."

The latent heat in her core began to simmer, and she inhaled slowly. "I will wear one of my dresses," she responded, and her cousin huffed in disappointment. If only she knew that Natalie did not have to wear a special dress to capture Jasper's attention. As these thoughts flowed in her mind, she discovered that she was growing excited.

She wanted to see Jasper again, and she wanted to spend as much time as she could with him. Only *him*. It was the simplest the truth had ever been.

Chapter Twenty-Five

※❦※

Some said that the Masked Rogue of London is hiding because someone saw the face of the Comtesse De Villepin. We must examine the life of every woman with red hair in London to find this woman. We know a few ladies with flaming hair in the aristocracy. Perhaps we should begin there.

Jasper folded the news sheet and frowned, staring blindly out the window behind his desk. He should have allowed Natalie to keep her wig. Placing masks on ships had been effective, but society was too inquisitive to let the matter rest. They would not stop until they had uncovered his face and Natalie's.

Jasper stroked his jaw slowly as he thought. There was already interest in Natalie, especially after Miss Gilmore decided that she had something to tell The Londoner. He swiveled his chair and drew a sheet of parchment from a stack before reaching for the quill.

MINERVA,

I hope this finds you well. I have a favor to ask of you, and I will visit you tonight. Please ensure that you are alone.

Sincerely,

MR

HE FOLDED THE NOTE AND SEALED IT, LEAVING THE WAX PLAIN. Then he called Smith and handed it to him. The valet needed only to glance at the name on the back of the note to know what to do with it.

"Wait for a response," Jasper instructed.

"Yes, Your Grace." When Smith opened the study door to leave, he encountered Wayne, and they exchanged a few words before he turned to Jasper. "The solicitor has arrived, Your Grace."

"Send him in," Jasper replied, reaching for the sheets that contained the particulars of his wealth that he only finished reviewing that morning.

The solicitor, Mr. Moore, walked in with his bag underneath his arm. He had done everything that Jasper requested but he never asked him why he was arranging his will, and even if he did, Jasper would not answer.

"I wish to add another name to the bequest list," Jasper said, sliding the papers across the desk to Moore.

The solicitor's eyes gleamed with curiosity, and he retrieved the list from the sheets he was handed. "May I have the name, Your Grace?"

"Lady Natalie Reeves." Jasper's heart twisted as he said her name. He had endeavored not to think about them parting, but he would have to face it at some point.

He wanted to depart knowing that she would want for nothing. It should give him some peace, at least. Jasper gave Moore instructions on what he wished for Natalie to have before he moved to the next matter he had called him for.

"I want to make an offer for the Earl of Clifford's townhouse. I heard he intends to sell it."

"Yes, that is the word about town, Your Grace." Moore scribbled onto a sheet. "Do you wish to inspect the property before offering?"

"Sight unseen," Jasper murmured. His breath was halting again, and he suspected that the thought of leaving Natalie was doing this to him. "I do not want the Earl to know who is purchasing the house. Use one of my businesses to carry out the transaction."

"It will be done, Your Grace. Would you like to negotiate a sum?"

Jasper shook his head. "I will make a very generous offer, and if he demands a greater sum, which is unlikely, it will be paid." He was sure that Clifford would not refuse the offer, considering the state of his affairs.

Upon winning against him at White's, several gentlemen had been interested in both gambling with Clifford and doing business with him, but that interest appeared to have waned very quickly, and Jasper found it curious. He would have to search for the reason, he decided.

THAT EVENING, PHOEBE SERVED HERSELF A GENEROUS AMOUNT OF brandy instead of the sherry she preferred to have after meals, and Jasper's eyebrows knit from his seat by the hearth. His aunt had been quiet throughout dinner, and her choice of beverage now added to Jasper's growing concern.

He left his chair to sit beside her on the sofa. "Are you well, Aunt Phoebe?"

"Oh, how can I be well when you saw it fit to exclude me from your meeting?" she answered with a small sniff and a rise of her chin. Jasper's frown deepened in puzzlement, but before he could ask her to elaborate, she said, "A will, Jasper? I thought we have talked about this. *Nothing* is going to happen to you."

"You heard what I discussed with Mr. Moore," Jasper said flatly.

"I was passing your study, and I could not help listening when I heard you mention a will and a name you wanted to include," Phoebe confessed. "People revise their wills often. This much I understand, but knowing the reason you are doing this pains me." Her eyes gleamed with emotion that shot into his heart like a bullet.

"I like to be prepared, Aunty," Jasper said softly. "Father and Grandfather were not. I suppose I am fortunate to have this chance."

"What are you preparing for? Death?" Phoebe asked impatiently. "One thing about death is that it never comes when one expects it," she added, her eyes shining with barely restrained tears.

Jasper wrapped an arm around his aunt and drew her close. "I am sorry, Aunt Phoebe. I know you want me to believe that this is not the end for me, and I truly wish that I could."

She released a shy breath and pulled away, surprising him when an unnaturally bright smile appeared on her face. She was denying what he had said, he knew, but he allowed her the liberty to have some cheer even if it was a false one. "I have decided to have garlands made of silk vines to decorate the ballroom. What do you think?"

Jasper smiled ruefully and kissed her cheek. "It is perfect." He knew she was anything but herself, and guilt scraped his insides for upsetting her. To make amends, he indulged her wishes for his ball. "Have you finished planning the refreshments?" he asked.

"Not yet. I wanted to ask you if you would prefer salmon and cheese on the canapés or cheese and cucumber?"

Jasper chuckled. "Why not both?"

"Yes, but you are not fond of cucumbers."

"Some of the guests are."

"I suppose you are correct. We will have every variation of the canapés Cook is capable of preparing." Her smile softened. "I am hoping that Lord Clifford, *Lady Natalie*, and Miss Reeves will attend."

Her emphasis and pause on Natalie's name did not escape his notice, and he allowed himself an inward smile.

"Do you not hope they will attend?" she asked, blinking expectantly.

"I am confident they will," he replied, noticing that her brandy was untouched.

"Splendid!"

"Do you not want to drink, Auntie?"

She proffered the glass. "No, I do not. Would you like to have it?"

"Certainly," he murmured and accepted it, gulping down half the contents. They conversed pleasantly for another hour before Phoebe retired, and he decided to call upon Oliver before proceeding to Minerva's house. She lived on Bloomsbury Street and it was not far from Oliver's residence.

He left the manor, and an hour later, he arrived at Oliver's townhouse. He was shown into the game room where his friend was playing billiards. Oliver raised one eyebrow when he saw Jasper.

"I could not quite believe it when the butler told me you had arrived."

"Why are you so surprised?" Jasper picked up a cue and chalked the tip.

"You rarely leave the manor after sundown." Oliver rearranged the balls so they could play a new game.

"You were gone for two years, and a lot has changed in England, myself included."

"Does that mean you will take a wife at last, so that you may give your dukedom an heir?"

"I believe there is an earldom in want of an heir, too," Jasper shot back, and they laughed.

"I did not know that you were well acquainted with Lord Clifford," Oliver said after he earned the right to be the first player. "I must admit that I am rather surprised by that development."

Jasper caught something odd in both Oliver's tone and expression as he mentioned Clifford. It was difficult for him to discern what it was, but it curiously reminded him of the tension he had observed the night before. *Puzzling*.

"I think Clifford is agreeable, and he plays piquet excellently."

"Do you already consider him a friend?" There was that oddness again. It was neither approval, nor disapproval, but it was strong enough for Jasper to take a great interest in.

"Yes, I do," he replied. "Is there a particular reason you are asking?"

Oliver shook his head and gestured for him to take his turn. "Only curiosity, my friend. Clifford is, indeed, a good gentleman, and I enjoy doing business with him."

A thought came to Jasper just then. It was something he had never thought of, and it laid the way for unsettling questions to rise. Why was Clifford failing if he was a good man to do business with? Why was Oliver doing well and not the Earl? He pondered the wisdom of asking Oliver about this, but he decided not to. It was not his business—in a way.

He left Oliver's house shortly after being outdone in the game and made his way to Minerva's.

Chapter Twenty-Six

Comtesse De Villepin is a very young woman. According to Baron Peckhart, she was made in the great image of Venus herself. Ladies and gentlemen, we now know to seek a beautiful red-haired woman. We are certain that once we find the Comtesse, we will find the Rogue.

Before Jasper went to Minerva's house, he stopped at his townhouse to don the black attire that the Rogue was known to wear. He wore his black mask at the door and proceeded to his destination.

Minerva opened the door herself when he arrived, and she tilted her red head and regarded him with curious gray eyes. "Why should I allow you into my house, MR?"

Jasper gave her a lopsided smile. "I came to apologize, Minerva."

"Liar." She rolled her eyes and stepped away from the door, letting him through. Jasper looked about the dimly lit house and listened. It was very quiet. "There is no one here as you requested," she said, locking the front door. Minerva came to stand in front of him, and he took in her appearance.

She was dressed to please him in a tight dress that seemed to hinder her breathing. Her bright red hair was heaped atop her head like a pyramid. Months ago, the sight of a woman dressed the way he wanted would have been enough to awaken his need, but his blood flowed slowly in his veins tonight.

He was here for a different reason. Minerva had been the only mistress he kept for more than three months, and he believed she could help him now. Like the others, she had never seen his face, and he had never stayed with her through the night.

She led him into a sitting room, and while he sat in a chair, she moved to a table where an arrangement of decanters sat.

"Are you still fond of gin?" she asked.

"That has not changed," he replied.

She brought him the liquor and sat on the arm of his chair, touching his rigid shoulders. As her hand moved down his chest, he shook his head. Understanding, she moved to the chair opposite him, displeasure turning the corners of her mouth downward.

"If you are not here for pleasure, what do you want, MR? Your note was most ambiguous."

"I was in earnest about the apology," he began. "I was a cad, and I should never have said those things."

At the time he ended their affair, he had accused her of attempting to unmask him, but he later discovered that she was innocent. Now, Minerva grinned in response to his words.

"I never dared to imagine the day the Masked Rogue would apologize for anything."

He raised one shoulder. "Well, it likely will never happen again." He took a small sip of his gin before deciding to have a large gulp.

"Then I accept your apology." She leaned back in her seat. "How may I serve you tonight?"

"I want you to be the Comtesse De Villepin."

Minerva sat up and stared at him, her lips parted in surprise. "Why ever would you make such a request?"

"It does not matter why but I am obligated to protect the actual Comtesse." Jasper believed Minerva's red hair and slight figure were enough to trick society.

"Why do you think me capable, MR?"

"You have the appearance, and you speak French." Her mother had been a French actress, and Minerva was raised in a theater. "You also possess the skill to fool society."

She laughed. "Those are quaint compliments, MR, and because you are so *charming*, I will oblige you."

"Good." He finished the gin and set the glass down, reaching into his coat to retrieve a mask. "You will require this."

"This Comtesse, she is important to you, is she not?" she asked as she took the mask, admiring the craftsmanship. When Jasper did not respond, she went on. "I have been reading The Londoner."

"The Londoner is often wrong."

"Yes, but you have never kept a woman for long. I have cause to think that your heart might have been captured."

Jasper had no wish to discuss Natalie, and he decided not to say anything more on the subject.

"Are we going somewhere tonight?" Minerva asked when she felt his resistance.

"Yes," he drawled.

A devilish smile curved her lips. "Then we better leave. The night is short."

"Natalie!"

The needle she was running through lace pricked her finger and she dropped both the tool and fabric, wincing. Then her head snapped up as Hannah appeared in the doorway of the sitting room upstairs. The gleam in her eyes was telling of the discovery she made.

What did Jasper do? "What did The Rogue do now?" she asked, feigning disinterest.

"The Comtesse. She made an appearance at Dale's last night." Her cousin showed her the page of The Londoner that mentioned both the Comtesse and the Rogue together.

Natalie stiffened, and it took a great measure of willpower to not react. Natalie did not go out last night. Who was with Jasper? "How interesting," she murmured, handing the sheet back to Hannah without reading the rest. She recognized the ill feeling forming inside her to be jealousy.

Why had Jasper taken another woman who had stolen her alter ego to the same place he took her? Did he pleasure her in his private room, too? She clenched her teeth and forced the thoughts out of her mind.

"That is all I came to show you," Hannah said as she folded the sheet. There was a knowing look in her eyes, and Natalie thought she would tell her that she knew who the Rogue was, or that she believed Natalie was the Comtesse and had snuck out of the house last night.

George walked into the room before Natalie could respond, and the instant he closed the door, her stomach clenched in dismay.

"I have something to tell you," he announced, looking from Hannah to Natalie, his expression betraying nothing.

"Is something the matter, Brother?" Hannah asked immediately, looking as uneasy as Natalie was feeling.

"We received an offer for this house," he said, sounding as though he was displeased.

Hope sparked within Natalie, but it was snuffed just as quickly when she recalled that the house no longer belonged to them. This must be what George felt.

"We cannot sell the house any longer because Father gave it to him," Natalie said in a monotone voice, forcing down the lump of disappointment in her throat.

"That is correct," George agreed. He appeared to contemplate for a moment before he added, "I have never seen an offer this generous."

Hannah winced. "Why are you telling us this? Dangle the carrot and pull it away."

"This house is ours, and you must know."

"Who made the offer?" Natalie asked.

George frowned. "I am unsure of who it is but the offer came from a business and not an individual."

"Can you not find out who owns the business?" Natalie wondered.

"It would be a waste of time since we no longer own the house," Hannah huffed and sank into a chair.

"It might not be a waste of time, Hannah," George said determinedly. "I intend to investigate the document Oliver showed me when he laid claims on the house. He did not leave it with me, but Uncle Hubert's solicitor should know something about it."

Her father's solicitor had retired a year ago, but hope sparked in Natalie's heart. If there was a chance that the house was still theirs, then she would encourage George to accept the offer.

"I cannot help but feel," he continued, "as if Oliver's claims are false. He will do anything to have us begging on the streets, especially lie."

"You said that you saw Father's signature on the agreement," Natalie remarked.

"I did, but it could have been falsified. We will know the truth soon."

Natalie and Hannah nodded at the same time that George made another announcement, withdrawing a note from his coat pocket. "The Duke of Amsthorne has invited us to attend his birthday ball in a fortnight."

Natalie sucked in her lips and looked away. She was confused about the Comtesse being out the night before, and why Jasper allowed it. But then she reasoned that he was not a man who acted without a purpose. There has to be a reason. *It better be a good reason.*

While Hannah got excited over the ball and followed George out of the room, Natalie forced a smile and pretended she was looking forward to the ball, too. In her heart, she prayed desperately for some light in their lives.

Several hours later, as Natalie was folding a dress she had finished mending, her gaze found The Londoner. She snatched it up and read the entire page, but she did not find the answer she sought there: the reason for Jasper's actions.

She also wondered when Hannah would finally confront her about it. Her cousin had purposefully refused to speak about the Rogue since Natalie went to gamble with him. The Comtesse was revealed the following day, thus, Hannah had to have solved the puzzle. Showing her the sheet earlier must have been an attempt at confirmation.

Natalie got to her feet and decided it was time she spoke to Hannah about it. She found her in her bedchamber getting dressed for dinner.

Hannah smiled when their eyes met through the vanity mirror. "Oh, good evening, Natalie."

Natalie acknowledged her greeting with a slight incline of her head. "Are we truly going to carry on with the game of silence, Hannah?" she asked.

"What game do you speak of, Natalie?" Hannah returned, lowering her gaze and coloring up. She reached for some flowers and tucked them into her dark hair. She had never been a convincing actress.

"Oh, you know very well what I speak of, Hannah," Natalie insisted, sitting on her cousin's bed.

"Very well," Hannah whispered her next words. "I know that Amsthorne is the Masked Rogue of London, and you are his Comtesse. I know everything!" Her eyes gleamed with the revelation, and her excitement translated into her bouncing in her seat.

Hannah might know everything, but she did not seem to know that Natalie was not the Comtesse that had been seen the night before. "Why did you keep quiet about it?"

"I know you wish to protect his face, and I did not want to say anything unless you want to talk about it."

Natalie smiled. It was most considerate of her cousin. "You did well. Did you write today's story?"

Hannah's head bobbed. "Oh, yes! Everyone thinks the Comtesse is the most beautiful creature to ever grace London!"

Natalie felt some heat rise to her cheeks despite her mood. "It is only because she speaks French, and she has bright red hair."

"Are all of those things not glamorous? It is what England sorely lacks. Most ladies look the same, and nearly every gentleman is seeking a blonde-haired and blue-eyed wonder!" She rolled her eyes at the last sentence. "The Rogue has excellent tastes."

Natalie found a small pillow and playfully tossed it at Hannah, and they laughed.

"We must be careful, now more than ever," she warned gravely. "No one can ever know about this."

"Of course! I will take this to my grave, Natalie," Hannah replied. "You can trust me."

"I trust you, Hannah." Natalie bit her lip before saying, "I won two thousand pounds through the games I played."

Her cousin's eyes enlarged. "Two *thousand?*"

Natalie grinned. "Yes, and I want to give a thousand to George to repay some of our debts while we share the other thousand."

Hannah immediately shook her head. "Oh, I cannot accept that. It is yours."

"And you are my sister. I want to share it, and I will not rest until you accept."

Her cousin chewed her lip as she considered. "I accept, but I want you to give George my share."

"Very well," she agreed. Their debts were monumental, but this sum would help them greatly. Natalie was tempted to gamble again but she quickly pushed the thought away. She had been lucky but that could change. George was excellent in every game of cards, yet he never risked their fortunes to make more. And there was good reason for it.

A knock came at the door, and Natalie answered it. The butler handed her a note. "This just arrived, My Lady. The messenger is waiting for a response."

This prompted Natalie to open it as soon as possible. "Give me a moment," she said, closing the door and walking to Hannah's bureau.

"What is that?" her cousin asked.

Natalie broke the wax seal and unfolded it, her heart leaping when she saw Jasper's penmanship.

My darling,

If you will accept, I shall come for you in two days to grant your fencing wish.

J.

. . .

"I AM FENCING WITH JASPER IN TWO DAYS," SHE SAID ABSENTLY TO Hannah.

"Oh, how marvelous that you use his Christian name!"

Natalie shook her head and penned a response that said simply: *I accept.*

Then she opened the door and gave the note to the butler. When she turned around, Hannah was giggling with a hand clapped over her mouth.

"What is it?"

"I feel terribly triumphant knowing something society can only dream of discovering."

"I should remind you that you were once at the fore of this ignorance and speculation, Hannah," Natalie teased.

Hannah dismissed her statement with, "Now that I know, I feel as if I am the Goddess of Knowledge. Allow me this victory, Natalie."

"You may have it." She looked down once more at the note from Jasper, and her insides fluttered. She yearned for him, but she also wanted answers.

Chapter Twenty-Seven

The Masked Rogue of London and the Comtesse De Villepin filled Dale's with revelry last night. According to Mr. Lupton, Sir Marcus Hiddleton has made the Comtesse a marriage offer. Unbelievable!

"Will the Comtesse accept Sir Marcus' proposal?" Hannah mused as they ate dinner the following evening.

"Sir Marcus likely made that offer while he was drunk," George said, raising his wine goblet to his lips.

"I have it on good authority that he did not drink at all that night." Hannah gave Natalie a knowing look. "He was simply besotted by the Comtesse."

George set his glass down. "Perhaps I should visit Dale's one of the nights the Comtesse makes an appearance. I would like to see her."

Natalie choked on the potatoes she had just attempted to swallow, and she began to cough profusely. George immediately placed a hand on her back, encouraging her cough, while Hannah stared at her with wide-worried eyes.

Natalie glared at her when she calmed, and George asked, "What happened?" Hannah bit back a laugh and looked away, forcing a large bite of potatoes into her mouth.

Natalie coughed again. "I ate too quickly. Do not worry, George."

He nodded and glanced at Hannah, frowning. "You should eat slower, sister." He turned back to Natalie. "As I was saying, I would like to see what the fuss about this Comtesse is all about."

"I heard she does not go out often."

"I shall have to take the chance." He grinned. "Who knows, maybe I might offer for her if I find her—"

"No!" Natalie and Hannah cried at once, and he looked from one to the other in confusion. "The Comtesse is not right for you," Hannah quickly added.

"Why not?"

Hannah's gaze met hers, and they quietly agreed to keep George away from Dale's. How they would go about such a task was another thing entirely. "Brother, you appear to have forgotten that she is the Rogue's mistress, and you are a nobleman."

"I thought you said the rogue could be a nobleman," George argued. He seemed to be earnestly curious about the Comtesse.

"He might be," Hannah answered, "but she is his mistress and you are an Earl. This is not done in our society."

He laughed. "I can still marry her and live in a cottage in Scotland or even France where no one knows me."

Now they knew he was jesting, and Natalie breathed out in relief. A sudden commotion in the front hall drew all of their attention before they could continue the conversation, and George shot to his feet.

He was about to go out into the hall when Oliver stormed into the dining room, with the worried butler on his heels.

"My Lord, I tried to tell him that you are dinin—"

"Be quiet, old man!" Oliver snapped at the butler.

"Do not speak to him in that manner!" Natalie interceded, giving the butler an apologetic look and a nod for him to leave.

"What do you want?" George demanded. "What gives you the right to barge into our home at this time?"

"Your home!" Oliver scoffed, turning hawkish gray eyes at Hannah. "I have come to collect what is owed to me, Clifford," he continued insolently, and Natalie moved to stand in front of Hannah, feeling her tense. She reached behind and took her cousin's hand, squeezing reassuringly.

"Nothing is owed to you in this house, Ecklehill. Now, if you have any respect left for yourself, you would leave quietly or—"

"Or you would have me thrown out?" Oliver interrupted with a laugh. "Of my own house? Need I remind you that your time under this roof is running out if you do not give me the compensation I demand?"

"How dare you!" Natalie spat. "Only a coward would touch his boot to the ribs of a man on the ground."

"You dare speak to me like that, Natalie?" Oliver glared at her.

"How else should I speak to you when your single objective in life is to torment my family?"

"Your father refused to give me what I truly wanted the first time, but by God, I will have it this time." He was referring to the marriage offer he made after taking most of their fortune. Her father had refused to allow him to marry Natalie and called him an evil demon for making such a request after what he had done to them. It wounded his pride and honor more than anything.

But Natalie would have rather died a thousand times than marry him.

Now he was back, and he wanted Hannah. She would rather die, too, than let him have her. "Do what you want, Oliver," Natalie ground out. "You will not marry any woman in this family." She said that with confidence that was only on the surface.

Hannah stared on in horror throughout this exchange, and Natalie felt the grip on her hand tighten. The fear she sensed in her cousin broke her heart, but it gave her the strength to maintain a brave stance before Oliver.

"You will regret saying that."

"No one will regret anything, Ecklehill. Now, get out of my house!" George bellowed, but Oliver was unmoved. He held Natalie's defiant gaze.

"You have always been a reckless one, Natalie. One's fortune is a thing never to be taken lightly. I have given you all a second warning, and there shan't be a third," he threatened before storming out of their house in a gust of exasperation.

Hannah broke into tears the instant they were alone. Natalie and George tried their best to comfort her, and after this, none of them could eat any more food.

"I need to know if this house was truly given to him," George vowed, and Natalie silently agreed with him.

Chapter Twenty-Eight

The Comtesse De Villepin is everywhere! Every theater, tavern, park, and gambling hell has a woman dressed as the Comtesse. We know the real Comtesse has never been seen without her Masked Rogue, but with every woman in London wishing to be her, our task of unmasking this mysterious woman has grown more difficult by a hundredfold.

It was the night that Natalie was going to fence with Jasper, at last, and Hannah was sitting on the bed while she dressed. George had sent word to Gloucestershire to her father's former solicitor, Mr. Alcott, and they had done all they could to comfort Hannah, but there was still a deep sadness in the depths of her eyes.

Natalie had felt guilty for going out to indulge her desires, but her cousin had encouraged her, telling her that she deserved to chase happiness no matter if Oliver was at their door like a bloodhound.

She wrapped the luxurious cloak around her shoulders and smiled at Hannah. "Have a grand time tonight," Hannah said.

"I will." Natalie slipped out of the house, and as soon as she stepped into the alley, a hand circled her wrist, and she gasped, her heart racing; not from fear but excitement, because it was Jasper.

He took her face between his palms and kissed her deeply. She still had questions to ask him, and she was still filled with jealousy, but Natalie allowed herself to melt in his arms for that moment. His mouth was warm in the icy night, and he sent sweet heat throughout her body.

"You cannot know how long I have been waiting to do that," he murmured against her lips before wrapping an arm around her shoulders and ushering her to the carriage while she smiled.

He helped her into the carriage, and after giving the driver instructions, he joined her, opening a small chest beside him on the rear-facing seat. "You need to be properly attired for tonight," he said, removing a jacket and a pair of breeches from the chest.

"You want me to wear that?" she asked as she took the fencing garments and examined them.

"Yes," he replied, quirking an amused brow at the surprise on her face. "The gymnasium we are going to admits men only. Although there is no one there at this time, I do not want anyone to suspect anything."

Natalie had overlooked the fact that she would need the proper outfit for the occasion. "I did not think of that."

"Never say you planned to fence in your dress, my darling." The endearing tone in his voice soothed some of her jealousy.

"You never know, Jasper. It could become fashionable for women to fence and do it in their dresses. After all, we live in an utterly fickle society," she giggled at his jest.

When she made to stash the clothes away, he held her hand. "You must wear them before we arrive. I should have sent them to you earlier but I forgot."

Suddenly feeling self-conscious, Natalie took off her cloak before reaching for the column of buttons on the back of her dress. As she fumbled with them, she felt Jasper sit behind her and his long fingers join hers. She sucked in her breath and closed her eyes momentarily, relishing his touch as her heart beat ever so quick.

Patiently, he helped her undo each button and unlace her stays. When he pushed the dress down her shoulders, the heat in the carriage rose. Her mouth dried, and her core pulsed sweetly. She looked at him over her shoulder, and his desire was evident in his gaze.

Jasper kissed her shoulder, and she sighed, turning. He stopped her and shook his head. "I might ravish you if you turn." His tone was light but she caught the small strain in his voice. He passed a white satin sash over to her. "You might want to bind your bosom with this for the jacket to look right."

"You wish for me to look like a man," she murmured, and he laughed.

"Never." He kissed her bare shoulder again. "You are more womanly than anyone I know. Look how you bewitched the entire town." This was her chance to ask him about the false Comtesse but then he asked, "Do you want me to help you?"

"Yes." Natalie handed the sash back to him and lowered her dress all the way to her waist so she could get out of it. Her stays, chemise, and petticoats followed before he began to carefully wrap the sash around her bosom. The silken fabric touching her breasts caused her nipples to stiffen, and she closed her eyes.

Natalie was glad she had her back to him, because his touch and closeness were making her color up. She did not need him to see her thusly.

"There." He reached for the jacket and helped her into it, and she wore the breeches herself before he returned to his seat, regarding her under-hooded eyes that told her a little about his thoughts. They wanted each other, but they would have to wait until after their sport, otherwise, they might never arrive at the gymnasium.

"I read about another Comtesse in The Londoner," she said, and he leaned forward, resting his elbows on his knees.

"Yes, I asked Minerva to pretend to be the Comtesse. To steer the vulturine eyes away from you," he explained.

It is to protect me. Still, the voice of doubt pushed her to question him further.

"Who is Minerva?"

"She was my mistress."

Natalie immediately regretted asking the question because she had more peace not knowing who he had been with that night. Now she could not help thinking of what they had likely done in his private room.

"You have no reason to be jealous of her, Natalie. She is no longer my mistress."

"I am not jealous," she said softly as she turned to look out the window.

"Well…I would have been jealous." He let out a small laugh. "There is no man in your life but I find myself jealous because I cannot bear the thought of any other man having you."

Natalie thought of admitting her jealousy, as well, but she decided against it. "Would your new Comtesse accompany you on your nights about town?"

Jasper shook his head. "No." He reached for her hand. "You, Natalie, are my only Comtesse De Villepin, and the reason I asked Minerva to pretend is so you would be protected. She has some influence in London, and many women she is acquainted with are dressing as the Comtesse to mislead society."

She could not help laughing, both from relief and in reaction to what he said. "London will be very confused."

"Certainly." He smiled softly. The carriage slowed, and looking out the window, he announced, "We are here."

Natalie looked out, and she was surprised to find an isolated atmosphere. The street was quiet and empty, and the gymnasium was a small building with a large sign bearing the image of pugilists and swordsmen.

Jasper led them through an obscure entrance on the side of the building and down a flight of stairs to the floor below ground. A man greeted them before handing him a key, and taking Natalie down a hall, he opened a door that led into a fencing chamber.

"Do you also reserve this room for your special use?" Natalie asked as she took in the room with wooden walls and all manner of fencing equipment.

"Convenient, hmm?" Jasper asked with a smug smile curving his lips, and Natalie giggled. He locked the door.

After giving her a mask, he allowed her the choice of weapon, and she selected a sword with a broad guard. Surprise fleeted over Jasper's features, but he remained silent.

Natalie took the weapon and felt its weight in her hand before taking position. "Have you fenced before, Natalie?" Jasper asked, looking almost intrigued now. "That blade is the heaviest of the three types of fencing blades, and you do not look as though you are handling it for the first time."

"Fencing was my father's favorite pastime, and I quite enjoyed my bouts with him. He taught me, you see. It is all fond memories now which is why I wished to try it once more," she explained.

"The surprises you come with never end, do they?" Jasper looked impressed.

"Stay with me for a while, and you shall find out," Natalie returned slyly.

"Let us play a game," Jasper proposed before he took his stance. "Whoever scores a point gets a chance to ask the other a question which they must answer with absolute honesty."

Natalie contemplated the wisdom in this before she nodded, ignoring the voice in her head that tried to convince her against it. She wanted to know why he was the Masked Rogue of London, and this was her chance.

Although she did not know how good a player Jasper was at the sport, she had decent skill. *I need only avoid losing,* she told herself just as Jasper took a lunge at her.

She parried immediately, and the move was not as impressive as she imagined it. Natalie had not fenced in a while, but she was happy to see that she still had a knack for the sport. She allowed herself a satisfied smile as she took her own lunge.

Jasper was unsurprisingly an impressive sport, but he complimented her. The next move she made was with more confidence, and it invited him to say, "At this rate, neither of us would get to ask those questions, and I am awfully curious about you."

"So am I." Natalie took a quick lunge that he did not defend in time, and she pointed her blade at his chest and scored.

"Splendid," Jasper chuckled. She thought he would complain but he gave her the point, saying she had earned it.

"I am very happy to be questioning you, Jasper," Natalie gloated, removing her mask.

"Do not get too happy," he returned before asking what it was going to be.

Natalie paused in thought. She'd had a question for him for a while now. One she had thought better of asking, but now that she was presented with the opportunity, she did not want to pass it up. It was not as simple as why he was the Rogue.

"What birthed the Masked Rogue, Jasper," she asked.

She saw him visibly tense, but he straightened his shoulders and took off his fencing mask with a sigh. "Obligation birthed the rogue, Natalie," he said, and she felt her brows crease in puzzlement. She was about to ask him to explain when he offered it to her. "My grandfather told his wife one afternoon that he had a headache, and that he wanted to sleep for a short while. He did not wake up from that slumber. He was thirty-five years old and in perfect health. How could he have died so suddenly?"

Natalie's chest tightened. "I am sorry, Jasper."

He gave her a ghost of a smile before continuing. "One week after my father turned five-and-thirty, he told me that he had a headache. I was ten years old at the time." He passed a hand over his brow, and Natalie went to him. He was reliving a painful memory for her sake. "I sent for some tea for him, but five minutes later, I saw him slump in his chair. He did not wake up." He held her gaze, and she realized that his story had answered her question.

"You think you might suffer the same fate."

"The same curse," he corrected, and Natalie never saw him more pained. What she thought was a coincidence seemed so real to him that he depended upon it, planned his life around it. His birthday was drawing near, and she could understand him becoming afraid.

"Is there a chance that it could be a coincidence?" she asked, her throat tight. Natalie did not want to believe he was cursed.

"My father and grandfather dying of the same mysterious condition at the same age? It is too precise to be coincidental. Whatever my fate, I owe an obligation to my family name," Jasper continued elaborating. "I need to leave it as pristine as my father and grandfather left it. Thus, I created the Rogue to live as freely as I could, and according to my own terms. The Duke is perfect, and the Rogue is the opposite."

It all made sense now, but Natalie's heart ached for him. The thought of losing Jasper arose a consternation so deep within her it pained. *No.* She *refused* to lose him.

"*You,* sir, are not going anywhere until we have finished fencing," she quipped, trying to find some levity in the grim situation.

Wearing their masks again, they carried on with their game, and when

Jasper scored, he grinned. "My moment has come," he declared, imitating her gloating earlier.

"What do you wish to know?"

His expression softened, and when he spoke, it was in the gentlest manner possible. "What happened to your hands?"

The question embarrassed her, but she answered honestly. "All of England knows that my family lives in genteel poverty. I happened to be very fond of sewing, and I began to make dresses. My friend May Lynch owns a shop on Bond Street, and I give her the dresses to sell for me."

Natalie sewed a lot lately, and she was having more than calluses on her hands. Her neck and shoulders ached from the strain, and her eyes sometimes felt dull and heavy.

Something passed over Jasper's features at her confession, and she wondered if she had told him too much. Would it make him see her as a lesser person now? As the thoughts circled in her mind like a flock of restless birds, she grew so self-conscious that she lost some concentration when they resumed their bout.

She took a step back to evade him, but she slipped and landed ungracefully on her right ankle. Natalie winced, and Jasper was quickly by her side.

"Are you hurt?" he asked.

"No, I only landed improperly. I am well."

He knelt and took her foot in his gentle hands despite her reassurances of being fine. Carefully, he examined the foot. It felt a little tender, but it was unhurt.

"An impressive, but rather clumsy fencer, I must say," Jasper gibed, clucking his tongue.

They had a bit of a laugh before Natalie realized how close to her he was when he rose. As if he had read her thoughts, he placed a finger beneath her chin and tilted her face up to his.

Jasper softly brushed his lips to hers before kissing her. Natalie's body took the reins, and she leaned into his touch, throwing her arms around his neck.

Chapter Twenty-Nine

When the Masked Rogue of London made his first appearance six years ago, we thought, "How difficult can it be to reveal the face of a man. He is only wearing a mask." We are sad to admit that we have been shamed. Not only has the Rogue revealed himself to be a cunning man without a heart, he brought us a Comtesse that now prevents us from sleeping at night. Sir Marcus is at the fore of the search, for he believes he has found his bride. Some argue that it is not done, but the poor man insists upon it. After all, she is a Comtesse!

Jasper pulled away from her, his eyes dark with the desire that reflected hers. "Give me a moment," he whispered before moving away to pick up the cloak he had draped over the chair earlier. He spread it on the parquet and took her in his arms again, undoing her clothes.

Natalie shivered when he exposed her bare and the cold air touched her skin, but his lips warmed her. Pushing the jacket off her shoulders, he unbound her breasts, inhaling when they fell softly. "You are truly magnificent, Natalie," he murmured, and she bit her bottom lip, reaching for him. She wanted him to quickly divest her of her clothing so she could feel his searing touch all over. He caught her hands and shook his head, chuckling, "Patience, darling." Then he glanced down at her breeches. "We must rid you of that first...slowly."

Bringing his mouth close, he brushed her lips before kissing a fiery path down her body, his hands unfastening the buttons. As he pulled it down her legs, he sank to his knees, kissing her belly, her feminine mound, and finally, her quivering sex.

"Jasper!" she mewled, grasping locks of his hair and raising one of her legs, but he did not oblige her by kissing her more as she expected. He withdrew and rose, his gaze caressing her body.

When the most wicked grin drifted onto his face, she knew he was going to rob her of her breath. He took one of her hands and guided it to her center, stroking gently. Then he placed her other hand on her breast. Leading her, they began a slow and unimaginably sensual stimulation of her body.

"Look at me, darling," he gently commanded, holding her eyes and stepping away from her. As he watched her pleasure herself, he removed his clothes and took himself in hand, stroking and matching his movement to hers.

A new sort of heat flowed through Natalie, and her movements grew more urgent. "Jasper," she breathed desperately.

"Natalie," he returned, his body straining.

When her trembles grew and her knees began weakening, he took her in his arms and replaced the hand at her sex with his, rubbing her languidly. This slowed her release, but a beautiful franticness took her. She grasped at his shoulders, her thoughts chasing the bounty his hands were holding ever so out of her reach.

He enjoyed the gratifying torment he was putting her through, and Natalie ground her teeth, vowing to do the same to him the instant she got the opportunity. Then, as if lightning had struck her, she froze, while passionate flames melted her body.

Jasper kissed her, murmuring, "That is it, darling, feel everything." And, "You are impossibly beautiful."

She did feel beautiful at that moment. He lowered them onto the cloak and held her close while her body calmed down.

Natalie was not looking at him, but she knew that he was smiling, likely because of what he had done to her. She glanced up at him to see if she had guessed correctly, and Jasper was indeed smiling.

Their eyes met, and he brushed her hair from her face, which she could not recall loosening. Warmth and tenderness filled her heart as she gazed at him. Seeing an opportunity, she sat up and smirked down at him.

"What are you thinking?" he asked, and she responded by looking down at his erect member. Catching her bottom lip between her teeth, she wrapped her fingers around him and stroked slowly, relishing the contrast between his rigidness and the smoothness of the skin.

"Holy God, Natalie," he swore and closed his eyes.

She giggled and brushed her thumb over his moist tip, her own body growing hot and hungry.

"What are you doing to me?" he rasped.

"What do you think, darling?" she returned daringly, continuing her soft strokes. Jasper thrust his pelvis up and gritted his teeth.

"You...want...revenge." He barely managed the words, and she recalled something from a French novel she read. Licking her lips, she bent and kissed his member. His hands were immediately in her hair, and he was grasping the locks between his fingers, his breathing labored. Feeling triumphant, she licked a trail from the top to the base. He hissed between his teeth. What he said was barely coherent, but she thought she caught the word, 'Please.'

She drew him into her mouth and sucked. His grip on her hair tightened, and he pulled himself out of her mouth.

"Natalie...I cannot allow you to do this to me."

"You did it to me," she grinned.

He closed his eyes, and when he opened them, they were filled with a desire so raw it called to her soul. "That is different. You could never understand how much I wish to be within you."

Natalie's lips parted, and she took a long breath, realizing that she wanted the same. "Will you do it if I request it?"

He frowned and sat up. "You do not know what you are asking."

"I do, Jasper. I have never been more certain of anything in my life."

As soon as she uttered the words, he pulled her on top of him and reached between them to rub his member against her. "Kiss me," he said, and the instant she touched her lips to his, he pushed into her.

She wrapped her arms around him, deepening the kiss. As her body stretched to take him in, her heart swelled with the emotion she had been fleeing from. Natalie had known of its existence for a while, but she was forced to acknowledge it now.

She barely felt the sting of being penetrated for the first time. It did not matter what he had done to her in the past. She loved Jasper, and that was never going to change. Everything she felt, she poured into the kiss while he sheathed himself within her and held her tightly.

She pulled away to breathe, and he took hold of her hips, saying, "Move with me." Natalie did as he guided her, and they were soon engrossed in each other's fervency. Every thrust made her body clench, and when she could no longer take more pleasure, she burst, calling his name as her head fell onto his shoulder. Almost immediately, he frantically withdrew from her and groaned, his body jerking under her.

"Natalie," Jasper whispered, pushing her damp hair from her face and looking at her. He looked as though he wanted to say something, but he only pulled her close and held her for a very long while.

This was the second time she was observing him do such, and although she could not understand what it meant, her emotions rose and tightened her throat. Tears stung the back of her eyes, and as much as she tried to keep them away, one tear rolled down her cheek. Thankfully, he did not see or hear anything that would have him questioning her.

Several minutes later, he ran a hand down her naked back and kissed her shoulder, before pulling away. "We should go," he murmured, kissing her lips.

Natalie smiled. The evening could not have gone better, despite the realization of her love and the hopelessness of it.

Jasper helped her get dressed before they left. Instead of returning her home, Natalie was surprised when he took them back to his manor. The household seemed to have retired, and they made their way quietly up the stairs, and through the dark hallways to a door.

When he opened it, she walked into a large suite that consisted of a bedchamber, a sitting room, and two other rooms.

"I recall you telling me about an item on your list. Would you like to complete it tonight?" Jasper asked as he locked the door and she shrugged out of her cloak.

"What item is that?" Natalie asked as she brought up a mental image of the list. She carried it with her in her reticule every day, and it served as a reminder for her to not allow anything to dampen her dreams.

She had found courage, and to lose it now would be asking to step in front of an oncoming carriage.

"You shall see," he responded before leading her into the bedchamber. Her eyes widened briefly as she took in the tastefully furnished room.

"Impressed?" He grinned.

"We are going toward it." She gave him a sly smile.

"Not yet? You wound me, Natalie," Jasper placed a hand on his chest. "Well, then perhaps this will get you there," he added as he retrieved a small wooden box from a table close to the hearth. It was intricately carved, and when he opened it, she gasped.

"Is that cheroot?" She gazed at the rows of cigars in the box. She had told him that smoking cheroot was on her list, and she thought he would have forgotten.

Now she knew what he was aiming for. The next on her list was to smoke cheroot and drink to her heart's content.

And smoke and drink they did. Because it was Natalie's first time smoking, she choked on her first few puffs and they had a good laugh about it before Jasper showed her how to do it properly. They made themselves comfortable on his bed afterward, and Jasper slung a protective arm around her, pulling her into the warmth of his body. She felt safe and hopeful. With this security, and the eventful night she'd had, came the overwhelming desire to rest her eyes.

As Jasper ran a soothing hand through her hair, she succumbed to her weariness.

JASPER WATCHED NATALIE SLUMBER PEACEFULLY ON HIS COVERS. HE wanted her here with him, and simply regarding her brought a lot of warmth and tenderness to his heart. He wanted her with him forever, he realized, and his heart started beating faster.

He was surprised to discover this, but he was more pained. He was leaving her, but he could still treasure every moment he had with her. He could find some happiness in his last days, even if it would be an illusion. He sat up to remove his boots, which he never bothered to earlier, and his eyes found her reticule lying on the edge of the bed.

He picked it up and walked to a table, but as he made to set it down, the oddly shaped thing tilted, and a small piece of paper slipped out of it. He put down the reticule and reached for the paper. It was folded with the writing outside, but he thought nothing of it until a word caught his attention; scandalous dress.

Curious, he unfolded the sheet, and a broad smile illuminated his face when he found that it was Natalie's list. They had completed nearly everything there, and he was happy that he had been able to do that for her. He laughed quietly when he saw her wish to swim in the serpentine.

He read, *Be truly wanted. Loved.* But before he could examine the remaining words, the final item on the list took his breath. *Ruin Jasper's reputation.*

He stared at the words in shock, unable to believe his eyes. He tilted the paper, hoping he read it wrong. Every second that ticked was agonizing, and Jasper reread the words over and over, willing them to change. *It cannot be... Natalie does not mean these words!*

What cause would she have to ruin his reputation? Had everything between them been a lie to her? Alas, the words were bold and clear enough to give him his answer.

Chapter Thirty

One of the many Comtesse De Villepins about town lost her mask while performing on stage in the theater. The face of the actress, Agath McDermont, was not unexpected, but now we know who is not *the Comtesse.*

It wasn't just the sense of betrayal that hit him—it was everything at once. Natalie was the only person he felt safe to confide in, to reveal his secret of who he truly was, something he wouldn't dare do with anyone else. And yet, for all he knew, her motives were malicious from the start.

Ruin Jasper's reputation.

Was that before or after she found out who he truly was? The identity of the *Masked Rogue*, that everyone wished to reveal? Was she one of those desperate reporters, in hope of exposing his identity? Or was there something else that she was after? The worst pain he had ever felt tore his heart to pieces, and Jasper took several breaths, thinking he could not bear it.

All this time, he was convinced that Natalie was different. Special. Her emotions appeared sincere, yet the words in her list indicated otherwise. He needed an explanation, but he couldn't face her right now. He needed to be alone, to gather his thoughts in place and focus.

"Jasper?" Natalie called from the bed, and he turned stiffly to look at her. She moved her hand over the bed, looking for him. Her eyes were still closed, and he folded the list and slipped it back into her reticule before walking back to the bed.

He stood over her, suddenly numbed by what he had seen. Natalie opened her eyes and sat up, pushing her hair from her face and looking up at him. "What time is it?" she asked groggily.

Jasper tried to maintain an even demeanor as he glanced at the clock on his nightstand and said, "It is almost three. It is quite late." He turned and started toward the door. "I will have a carriage readied for you."

He found Smith and gave him instructions, and when the carriage was ready, he returned to find Natalie ready to leave. She looked tired, and he quickly reprimanded himself for noticing such. Keeping his tone even so she would not question him, he led her out of the manor and helped her into the carriage.

Natalie was a clever woman, and his cold cordiality did not escape her, because when their eyes met, he saw the question in them. He wanted her to leave so he could gather his thoughts and understand what he had seen.

"Are you all right, Jasper?" she asked.

"Yes, I am," he responded, his voice sounding unnatural and distant. He could not help it. She regarded him with some skepticism in her eyes before adjusting her cloak.

"Good night then," she murmured.

"Yes." Jasper closed the carriage door and gave Smith a nod.

Then, he stared at it as it pulled away, anger and hurt snaking ruthless tentacles around his heart and squeezing until he bled.

He had been the greatest of fools to so recklessly give Natalie his trust. He walked back into the manor and went straight to his study, locking the door. He needed to be alone, and because he did not know how long he would require, he decided to have the door locked.

His jaw tightened as he sat behind his desk, and with a groan so pained it did not sound human, he swept everything that sat atop his desk with his arm, cursing. Papers, ink, figurines, they all fell to the floor in disarray; quite like his battered heart and shattered hopes.

※

Jasper's heart was still in pieces the following evening, and he was having great difficulty fathoming the last item he had read on Natalie's list.

Why had she been out to destroy his reputation? What did he ever do to her to deserve such?

Contemplating this was painful enough that he could not imagine what the answer would do to him. Yet the questions continued to choke him. Had everything between them meant very little to her? Had it all been an act from the beginning?

An act I was foolish enough to give my heart and soul to, he thought bitterly, refilling his tumbler with unsteady hands and spilling some of the liquor on his desk. He blinked at it, his vision terribly unfocused, but he did not care. Nothing mattered anymore. Not after he had lost the one thing that meant everything to him: Natalie.

A knock came at his study door, and Jasper did not trouble himself to respond. He had spent the entire day here. "Jasper?" Phoebe called. This must be the fifth time she was coming to knock on the door and call his name. Or was it the sixth? "Please open this door. I need to speak with you."

"There is nothing to say, Auntie!" he slurred. "I am well."

Phoebe shook the door, and when the sound annoyed him, he shot to his feet, grasping the back of his chair to steady himself when he swayed. He staggered to the door to unlock it, but not before he had fumbled with the lock for what felt like an entire minute.

His aunt clapped a hand over her mouth when she saw him, her eyes looking stricken. "What happened to you? You have been locked up in here for more than a day, Jasper." She stepped into the room while he staggered to sit in his chair by the fire. "You refuse to talk, you refuse to eat," she went on, and he could hear the concern and fear in her voice, and it caused him to wince.

When he did not respond, Phoebe dragged an ottoman and sat in front of him, touching his forearm. "Jasper, tell me what is wrong with you. *Talk* to me. Please," she implored, taking his free hand and clutching it tightly.

"Why does trust carry so much, Auntie?" he asked at length, not quite recognizing his voice. He had given Natalie his heart, and with it, his trust. That thought had been scraping his insides all day, and it continued to torment him.

Phoebe's frown deepened in confusion and concern. "Is this about Natalie? Was she the woman you had over last night?" On seeing the question in his eyes, she added, "Yes, the servants spoke of seeing a woman in the house, but no one knows who she is."

Jasper did not respond to his aunt's question, for he had nothing to say. Or rather, he did not know how to say it. He did not know how to share his broken heart.

"You love her, do you not?" Phoebe continued when his silence grew.

"It does not matter," his voice came at last.

"Oh, but it does. More than anything," she countered. "One cannot be without their heart. Whatever the situation, do not give up on yours, Jasper. Please." She squeezed his hand and placed a gentle kiss on the back.

He had not been sure whether he ever truly had that heart in the beginning, but whatever game Natalie had played, it was revealed to him now that he did possess a heart. Phoebe left him when he did not say anything, and an hour later, he dragged himself out of his study to visit Oliver.

He had a bath and dressed, then he rode to Westminster city to his friend's house. Oliver knew that something was wrong the moment he saw him. "What happened to you?" he asked.

"Fancy a boxing bout?" Jasper asked instead of answering.

Oliver nodded, and they walked into his game room which had enough space to spar. They took off their coats and began. Jasper noticed that his friend's aggression matched his, almost as if he was attempting to release his frustrations too.

After a few more moments of being in a deadlock, Jasper delivered a powerful punch that Oliver was barely able to defend. He staggered backward and nearly lost his balance.

"Bloody hell! If I did not know you very well, I would say that you have some sort of grievance with me, Jasper," Oliver panted. "I cannot recall ever seeing you like this. Is it a woman?"

Jasper mumbled an apology before asking, "What gives you the notion that it is a woman?" Jasper had asked that to stall his answer.

"Only two things make a man look as utterly defeated as you do now." Oliver wiped his brow with his shirt sleeve and raised a hand, counting. "Money and women. Last I looked, you have more wealth than you know what to do with. So, that leaves us with the latter. Who is she?"

Jasper heaved a sigh before he told him about Natalie, leaving out her list. Oliver regarded Jasper with a curious glint in his eyes as he spoke about her. In fact, his friend had a sudden look of expectancy that Jasper could not understand.

"Do you intend to court her?" Oliver asked. When Jasper gave no answer, Oliver mused, "Well, perhaps she is not the right woman for you."

Jasper had always appreciated Oliver's opinions and advice, and he had to admit to himself that he might be right. However, he was greatly conflicted. Where Phoebe had advised him not to give up on his heart and happiness, Oliver had countered that now. He did not know what to do anymore.

Jasper sat and allowed his head to hang. It ached from all the liquor he had drunk but he barely felt it amidst the chaos in his soul. He loved Natalie. He inhaled sharply because the discovery was powerful enough to knock him off his feet had he been standing.

The most surprising thing of all was how he wanted her to keep the heart he had given her, despite the ills she harbored against him.

Chapter Thirty-One

Ah, we see what has been done! The ever-elusive lovers had many women dressing as the Comtesse to hide the real one. Never you mind, London, we have better news today. The Duke of Amsthorne shall be hosting a grand winter ball to celebrate his birthday. Every person of consequence is invited. Now we know what you all are thinking, and we shall keep our eyes on the matter for you. This may be the final chance.

Natalie had not been able to stop thinking about the coldness she had perceived from Jasper when she woke from her short slumber in his manor. Had she perhaps imagined it? Or was she merely feeding her fear that should not be fed? She hoped it was the former.

After a fortunately uneventful dinner, George sat in the drawing room with Natalie and Hannah. "I made the acquaintance of merchants and gentlemen interested in investing in the factory," he told them. "It is to enable me to buy some of the portion of the business that Oliver controls. Unfortunately, they have lost interest in the endeavor."

"All of them?" Hannah asked, shifting uncomfortably in her seat.

"Not a single one remains," George responded ruefully. "I proposed another venture, and they turned it down too." He shook his head. "I cannot understand how they can claim interest and then change."

Natalie found it odd that they all withdrew at once. She recalled Oliver's threats, and could not help the suspicion that flooded her thoughts. "Do you think that Oliver might have discouraged them without you knowing?" she shared.

"It could be," Hannah agreed. "George, you have to find out." She was still being courted by Wessberg, thankfully, and they were all expecting him to offer before Oliver moved against them again.

Natalie agreed to this before asking George if he had received any word from the solicitor regarding Oliver's claims on their house.

"No, I have not heard anything from him. I," George sighed. "I will be patient."

Every day, their hopes were forced to decline, and the darkness they faced seemed unending. Natalie only prayed that they would have something left of them when all this was over.

George stood. "I will be in my study."

When they were alone, Hannah moved to sit beside Natalie. "You do not look well. What is the matter?" Natalie started denying but her cousin cut her off with, "Your eyes are glazed over and you look very pale. You have been like this all day."

"It is nothing, Hannah," Natalie lied. "I am only this way because of all that is happening."

"I do not believe that, Natalie," Hannah insisted. "I know when something is wrong. I *know* you."

"Well..." Natalie sighed, but she was still unable to tell Hannah what bothered her because she was unsure of what exactly it was.

"Did you perhaps quarrel with Amsthorne?" Hannah asked, and Natalie did not know how to answer without sounding ridiculous. That there had been no quarrel, only that Jasper suddenly seemed withdrawn after sharing a passionate night with her?

He usually told her, when saying farewell, that he would see her again, but he made no such pronouncement this morning. No word came from him today, and she was forced to wonder if he regretted their time together.

The thought twisted her heart, and she forced down the rising lump in her throat.

"Oh, you did have a disagreement," Hannah observed ruefully.

"It is nothing of consequence, Hannah," Natalie reassured for lack of more reasonable words to put in.

Hannah wrapped an arm around her, and Natalie swallowed, her emotions churning. "I tell you this as a writer whose one of many intrinsic qualities is keen observation," Hannah said. "Amsthorne cares for you. I have witnessed enough of your exchanges to be certain of this, Natalie."

"Thank you, Hannah." Natalie rested her head on her cousin's shoulder, appreciating the comfort.

"My advice is that whatever it is, give it time. Wessberg is a very quiet gentleman, and I often guess what his thoughts might be. I know he cares, and I am learning to be patient with him."

Natalie smiled, but despite the words of reassurance, the shadow of unease remained, hovering above her.

***

Ten days passed without word from Jasper, and it gave Natalie the dreadful certainty that he regretted their time and that he no longer wanted her. She filled her days with sewing, and when night came, her sleep was fitful.

Her dreams were only of Jasper, and while some delighted her, most plunged her into a pool of fear and apprehension. She was especially lost because of the love she had for him.

She walked into the drawing room this morning to the sight of George and Hannah's grim faces. She was about to ask them what happened when George held out a sheet. Her heart racing, she accepted it and discovered it was The Londoner.

This stretched her nerves further, and she began to read:

We know the reason Lady Natalie Reeves never married all these years. It was not her lack of dowry, and although she is pretty enough to be wed without one, the truth is far more sinister than any of us could have imagined. Ten years ago, when Lady Natalie was only nineteen, she was ruined by a gentleman.

Her father, the late Earl of Clifford, did not confront the gentleman. He was too old and drunk to care, and many gentlemen of the ton became aware of this. Now, we cannot tell how this news remained hidden all these years, but the gentlemen knew of the lady's taint and sought to keep away.

Trembling, she read the news over again, unable to believe the lies in it. One thing stood certain, though, and it was the fact that those lies had Oliver's name all over them. She would know the Earl's horrid words wherever she saw or heard them. This was doubtless his vile creation.

"Ecklehill! That bastard!" George's fist came down upon the table in front of him as Natalie lowered the sheet. His suspicions mirrored hers, it would seem.

Oliver is finally following through with his threats, Natalie thought miserably. She did not want to think of what he might have in store for them next, because he seemed relentless in his quest to destroy them. Ten years later, and he was as destructive as the first day.

"What do we do now?" Hannah asked, her eyes shimmering with wet tears.

Before George could put in a word, Natalie began to apologize for everything. "This is all my fault," she said, tears burning at the back of her eyes.

"Don't you say that," George and Hannah chorused before Hannah stood and wrapped her arms around her. George rose, too, and took one of her hands. Their tenderness and understanding forced the tears that Natalie had been keeping a tight hold on.

The butler interrupted them with the announcement of a caller. She wondered who it was, and thought it might be someone who had come to gather more gossip about her now that her name was smeared over every news sheet in town.

Then the butler said, "The Honorable Lady Phoebe Dawson."

She was relieved to hear that but it was fleeting as worry settled within her. She thought of the prospect of Phoebe reading the news and coming to cut ties with her.

"Show her in, please," George said, and a moment later, Phoebe walked into the drawing room.

She smiled at all of them, and after a pleasant exchange of greetings, George and Hannah left them alone. Phoebe did not mention the scandal, nor did she regard Natalie any differently.

"How have you been, my dear?" she asked Natalie, surprising her.

"I...I am well," she lied, wearing a false smile.

Phoebe glanced down at her hands, and the corners of her mouth turned downward. "I wish I could tell you the same, dear." She raised her eyes to Natalie. "I am worried about him, my Jasper."

Phoebe was not here because of the gossip, and certainly not to cut ties with her either, but the mention of Jasper wrung Natalie's heart. For the life of her, she could not understand the reason for his silence. She had sent him a note over the past days, but no reply had come.

"I do not know what happened between you two, but whatever it is, do not give it triumph over your heart, Natalie," Phoebe said gently. "He cares for you... More than you realize." She smiled at Natalie.

Does he really? Natalie thought as she sucked in her lips. Phoebe's words should reassure her but they both confused and tore at her. Why was Jasper miserable when he was the one who decided to stop seeing her? Was he keeping her away because of the fate he feared he would suffer at thirty-five?

"Doubt is the heart's greatest enemy, you see," Phoebe said as though she had read Natalie's thoughts right then. She placed a warm hand over Natalie's. "I read The Londoner this morning." There was no disappointment or judgment in both her tone and demeanor, but Natalie's stomach still sank. "I want you to know that I do not believe a word of those lies. Society's cruelty knows no bounds, and I know from experience that the instant they find something better, they will forget."

Natalie managed a smile. "Thank you for your kindness, Phoebe." She dreaded the question she was about to ask but she needed to know. "Has he read the paper?"

She would have no chance in Jasper's eyes, much less his heart, if he saw the sheet. He would remember the incident from ten years ago, her foolishness, and its insignificance to him. And like he did before, he would bury the past weeks they had shared without an ounce of sentiment. Natalie would once again be a forgotten memory with less meaning than a passing breeze.

Some of these thoughts were her doubts and fears, but she felt everything deeply regardless.

Phoebe gave a relieving answer. "No, he has not. I had all the sheets that were delivered to the manor this morning burned. I doubt he would see it because he has locked himself up in his study and wants no communication with the world."

He had locked himself up? Why? Nothing made sense. Why was he putting them both through this meaningless torture?

Chapter Thirty-Two

Some talk in hushed whispers but we do not do that at The Londoner. Many condemn us for our honesty. 'Ungraceful' they call it. Nevertheless, we will be watching the Duke of Amsthorne and Lady Natalie Reeves. This ball will tell us whether or not Miss Gilmore told us the truth.

Two days after Phoebe's visit, they received a second invitation for a ball from Jasper, but she was certain that this courtesy had come from Phoebe, because firstly, he was still playing his game of silence, and secondly, Phoebe wanted a chance for them to reconcile, and this invitation was as much a reminder as it was an encouragement.

"I am not attending," Natalie said on the morning of the ball. George and Hannah were also aware that something had gone wrong between her and Jasper, but they did not talk to her about it.

"Hiding would only give credence to those lies, Natalie," George said, and Hannah nodded in agreement. "We must keep our head up and face society."

She *did* want to see Jasper, if only to hear the true reason for his actions from his mouth, but she was also pained. After considerable thought, she decided to attend the ball.

Thus, at sundown, they departed for Amsthorne Manor. The exterior was bright with sconces illuminating the beautiful scopes, and the ballroom would have taken her breath away had she been in a better disposition. Phoebe and Jasper had gone to great lengths to host such an event, and she was sure that it would be talked about for a while.

Wessberg asked Hannah to dance as soon as they arrived. George was reluctant to leave her, but after Natalie's encouragement and reassurance that she would be fine, he went to investigate the reason his investors had withdrawn their interest. Many of the gentlemen were present tonight, and he must use the opportunity.

None of them had seen Jasper, and Phoebe had been too occupied with her hostess duties for Natalie to ask her any questions. It was as though he was not at his own ball. Ignoring the curious and even accusing glances and whispers directed at her, Natalie placed herself in one corner of the room, plucking a glass of champagne from the tray of a passing footman. After all the weeks of rebuilding her self-esteem, it had all shattered once more and she found herself in the place she had been for a long time.

The atmosphere suddenly changed, and she did not need to look up to know that Jasper had made an appearance. All the way from across the room. And while he was unaware of her, and she was not looking at him, he commanded her heart to long for him.

Jasper seemed all but pleasant as he made rounds greeting his guests. He smiled, and even laughed with some of them. He seemed to have mastered appearing untroubled. When he turned and their gazes finally met, her heart pounded violently. His eyes narrowed briefly before he turned his attention back to his guests.

She would have been happier if he had not seen her, for the coldness and lack of acknowledgment bit her like the deadliest of frosts. Natalie forced the bitter taste of hurt down her throat just as a shadow appeared before her.

God, help me!

She raised her eyes to meet Oliver's smug smile. "I must confess that I did not think you would have it in you to show your face in society, Natalie. But then, it takes a shameless person as much as a naive one to do what you did ten years ago." He laughed derisively.

"I suppose one can say that we are alike in that regard," Natalie returned, watching his face color with anger. He brushed a lock of blonde hair from his forehead and sneered at her.

"I assume your first dance is reserved for Amsthorne," he suddenly said with a knowing and mocking look in his eyes.

"It is no business of yours to whom I give my dances." Natalie's gaze inadvertently swept the ballroom, searching for the man in question, but Jasper had, once again, disappeared.

"I doubt he would ask you to that dance." He leaned in and lowered his voice to a whisper, "You see, Natalie, little by little, everyone around you is discovering your true nature, and very soon, you will be deserted. Believe me, my dear, it will be worse than your spinsterhood." He straightened quickly and said in a rather loud and unnaturally cheery tone, "It is indeed a pleasure seeing you here, Lady Natalie."

This drew curious glances in their direction, most of them full of judgment. Natalie felt an unpleasant chill run through her, while Oliver grinned in victory. He turned on his heels and left her there, to be skinned raw by the *ton's* disapprobation.

Unable to bear it, she found the first door that led out of the room, then she walked down the hallway without direction, seeking sanctuary. She saw a door that looked familiar and opened it. When she stepped into the room, she realized it was the same salon that Jasper had brought her to the night he hosted her family for dinner.

Closing the door behind her and resting against it, she closed her eyes, willing her racing nerves and warring emotions to calm down. Tinkling across the room made her stiffen, and she opened her eyes to see Jasper holding a tumbler with some liquor in it.

His surprise was a reflection of hers, but something shadowed his features. Natalie stared at a cold man whom she barely recognized. There was no trace of the man she had shared much warmth and tenderness with in the past weeks, the man she loved.

"I did not know the room was occupied," she heard herself say, her chest tightening. Natalie took a tentative step forward.

"You can make use of it," Jasper replied before walking past her to the door.

"Jasper, wait!" She reached for his sleeve, grasping it and stopping him. She needed answers so that her heart may stop aching.

There was no life in his eyes as he regarded her. "What more do you want, Natalie?" he asked impatiently, and for the first time, she saw movement in his eyes. Pain.

"I do not understand, Jasper—"

"Of course, you would not," he scoffed, and she endeavored not to wince at his palpable sarcasm.

"Did I do something wrong?" she asked.

"I should be asking *you* that." There was a slight tremor in his voice, and she was allowed to see the anger in his eyes now. "I should be asking you why you have not yet destroyed Jasper's reputation."

Her world began to fall apart all over again. "Oh my God!" she breathed.

"Yes. I saw the list. It fell out of your reticule," he responded.

"Jasper, allow me to explain—"

"I have read all the explanations I need on that list, thank you."

"But—"

"But what, Natalie?" he interjected, looking at her with disbelief. Natalie had never seen anyone look like that before. He was…broken?

Quite as you felt ten years ago, her mind's voice reminded her. It did not matter, because she did not care about his sins anymore. She wanted him back, and a quest for revenge had now cost her everything.

"You want me ruined, do you not? You have made that clear enough on your list. What more could you possibly have to say?"

He was right. She had nothing to say. Her defense would be that she had changed her mind because she had fallen in love with him, but he would not believe her. The stark truth was that she had once been determined to ruin him.

He reached for the door handle but stopped and turned to her. "Although…I am curious to know why you never followed through with your plan. Did I discover the truth before you could?"

"Jasper, please," Natalie tried again to make him see reason, but he would not listen.

"Were you leaving it until you were sure to inflict the most pain? You probably did not anticipate your vile plan being found, did you?"

"Vile plan?" Natalie bristled. "You have no right to speak of me in such a manner." The anger she had kept locked away from ten years ago broke free. He felt betrayed upon seeing her list, after forgetting what he had done to earn a place there.

"Indeed, I have no right." He surprised her with that statement. "I never had any right with you because everything was all a ruse to you, Natalie. There was never a moment of truth." The pain in his eyes returned, and without giving her a chance to respond, he opened the door and stalked out of the room.

When Natalie looked down at her hands, she found them shaking. She was trembling all over, and the journey to find a seat felt long and cruel. She fell into the chair, and her hands went up to cover her face. Shame, heartbreak, dishonor, she felt them all.

She was not sure how much time had passed when she finally gathered herself and wiped her silent tears. Rising, she decided to return to the ballroom to find her cousins so they could leave, or rather, so she could leave. Natalie could not bear the evening any longer.

George was in the ballroom hallway, and he was having an aggravated conversation with Oliver. "You should have thought of the consequences, you incompetent fool!" Oliver was saying to George.

"Watch your words, Ecklehill!" George warned, clearly trying to rein in his ire.

"Or what? Your ineptitude is no secret in society, Clifford," Oliver carried on taunting.

"What is going on?" Natalie stepped in. Oliver threw her a venomous glare before he returned his attention to George.

"You have failed in every manner. You have a sister and cousin you have been unable to marry off." Oliver gripped George's coat lapels and pushed him against the wall. "You will give me what I demand!"

"Devil take you!" George groaned, and before Natalie could blink, George and Oliver were exchanging blows. Guests poured out of the ballroom and gathered around them, some gasping, some whispering, and others staring with both interest and shock. No one made to intervene, however, and Natalie sought an opening to help her cousin.

Oliver struggled and gasped for breath as George caught him in his middle. He rained insults upon Natalie and Hannah, which further enraged George, and he pinned him to the wall, mindlessly shoving his fist in Oliver's face.

Natalie gripped his shoulders and tried to pull him back. "That is enough, George!" she cried. He pushed Oliver onto the floor, then turned to face her. "Oh, George!" His right eye was red from a blow, and his lip was cut and bleeding.

Natalie took his arm and tried to pull him away, but Oliver gained his feet and charged at him again. Their blows became more combative, and Natalie had to step away helplessly lest she got injured. Hannah found her, and they anxiously held each other's hands. Phoebe appeared and tried to enter the fray, but Natalie stopped her.

"No, they will hurt you. I tried." She felt a dull ache in her side as she said that, and she realized that she must have been hit when Oliver and George's brawl resumed.

Phoebe ignored Natalie and tried again, but she pulled her away at the same time that George crashed into a side table, breaking the vase on it. Oliver, whose face was quickly swelling, took hold of her cousin's collar, but then a commanding voice gave him pause.

"Damn you both!" Jasper bellowed as the crowd parted for him to reach them. "What is the meaning of this?" He disregarded George and turned to Oliver. "In my home? During my ball?"

Alexandra sidled up to Natalie then, saying, "I see you have animals in your family."

Natalie did not spare her so much as a glance. She took George's arm and helped him straighten, and deliberately refusing to look in Jasper's direction, she led him away. It was over.

Chapter Thirty-Three

Oh, Miss Gilmore informed us correctly. We saw quite the tension between the Duke of Amsthorne and Lady Natalie Reeves at the ball. Perhaps the Duke knew of her history and it was why he rejected her. Our heart goes to the poor lady, regardless.

Jasper watched Natalie lead Clifford away with Miss Reeves behind them. Seeing her had torn him to bits. So much so that he had not been able to stand being in the ballroom for long.

He had escaped soon to drown his woes in his cups, only for her to follow him, and eventually leave him eviscerated by their conversation. And when he thought his night could not get worse, Jasper heard a commotion in the hall and hastened to the horrendous sight of a brawl between Oliver and Clifford. Two friends of his that he never had believed capable of such.

What appalled him more than anything was the fact that society just stood by and watched the two gentlemen practically try to kill each other.

"My study, Ecklehill. *Now*," Jasper said to Oliver before he walked past him. He saw how swollen Oliver's face was when he entered the study, but Jasper was too angry to pity him at that moment. "What the devil was the meaning of that display?"

"You should have put in some thought before you invited just anyone to your ball, Jasper," Oliver hurled back, and Jasper's brows rose.

"I beg your pardon?"

"The Reeves are bad society. I never liked your relationship with Clifford."

Jasper clenched his jaw, wondering if Oliver knew anything about Natalie's plan. "Yet you never mentioned anything about this," he pointed out.

"Because I did not want to alarm you without cause," Oliver replied. "I intended to wait until I was sure they posed danger to you."

"But why did you see it right to engage Clifford in a fight at my ball like a pack of wild animals," Jasper threw back. Oliver knew how much he hated fights.

"Are you seriously taking his side, Jasper?"

"I am taking no one's side. Give me a damn reason!"

Oliver groaned. One of his eyes had already closed and the bruise around it was turning purple. "He started it. Clifford *strangled* me against the wall. I had to defend myself!"

Jasper recalled the tension he had sensed from the two gentlemen the night he hosted them. Whatever had pushed them to fight tonight was deeper than he thought. No one knew about Natalie's list, and it was likely not the reason Oliver thought them bad people.

"If you are having trouble with him because of your business, I would appreciate it if you kept me, and most definitely my guests, out of it," Jasper said.

"You think this is about business?" Oliver scoffed.

"Then what the devil got you two beating up one another in my home?" Jasper asked, growing exasperated. Oliver was not answering his questions directly.

His friend reached into his coat pocket and removed a folded sheet. "I was going to show you this after the ball to warn you about the family. They want only your fortune."

That did not make sense because Natalie had insisted upon giving him a hundred guinea from her winnings the first night he took her out. Not knowing what to expect, Jasper unfolded the sheet and read.

Natalie's name was painted red by The Londoner. The news about the scandal sounded familiar but he still did not know what to make of it. His heart beat faster, and his gut clenched. *Natalie compromised? How?*

"You *still* do not remember?" Oliver asked.

"What am I supposed to remember?"

"That night ten years ago when I dared you to kiss a debutante?"

The memories, as fragmented as they were due to him being drunk that night, rushed to the surface, and he tensed. "What? ...Was that Natalie?" He already knew the answer but he was anxious for Oliver to tell him that it was not her.

"Yes," he confirmed, hitting the nail on the head. "Natalie was that lady I chose and dared you to kiss."

Oh God! Jasper could not breathe. She had been compromised by him that night, and because of it, no one wanted to marry her.

"Clifford was here with a motive against you tonight. When I found out, I tried to defend your honor," Oliver continued. "We did a harmless thing. You did not even kiss her. No one was there."

Yes, only the three of them knew. *Wait!* "There was no scandal ten years ago," he said. "You were the only other person in the room."

"There could have been a scandal had I not stepped in and salvaged the situation," Oliver responded, sounding boastful.

Jasper glanced down at the gossip sheet still in his hands, wondering how the information had gotten out there. The only way would have been if Oliver, their only witness, had given it to them. *It cannot possibly be.* Oliver was more a brother than a friend to him. He would not betray him nor strive to ruin an innocent lady's reputation in such a manner.

"If you ask me, the price I demanded was too little for the work I did to protect Natalie's reputation," Oliver continued, his tone proud. He seemed a different man altogether.

"The price you demanded?" Jasper questioned slowly.

"Well, the coal business was nothing, really. Late Clifford was a stubborn old man, but it was that or his daughter's reputation. At least he had the wisdom to choose the latter."

"Did you blackmail Natalie's father with that stupid prank?" Jasper was in utter disbelief.

Oliver regarded him with surprise. In fact, his friend looked as though he was only just realizing that he confessed.

"Tell me what you did!" Jasper's gut clenched with dread. "Did you give this to the press?" He raised the sheet.

Oliver blanched, but then disdain gleamed in his eyes. "I needed the money then, Amsthorne. I saw an opportunity, and I took it." There was no remorse about him.

"Good Lord, Oliver!" Jasper let out in shock.

Was the man before him at this very moment truly Oliver Bargrave? His dearest friend? *Mayhap I never knew him, and he is only revealing himself.*

"Was the coal business the only thing you got from the late Earl?" Jasper asked, but he got the sense that there was more.

"I kept that scandal behind the curtain. What is a petty coal business? Of course it wasn't enough! I needed more," Oliver replied.

It all was becoming clear now. Oliver was the reason George was in heavy debt. The reason society lost good regard for him. And Natalie... *Dear God, Natalie!* He understood her grudge against him. She must have thought him responsible for the blackmail, too. Not only had the prank he thought innocent robbed her family of their prosperity, it made her a spinster. He braced a hand on his desk as a wave of guilt and torment hit him.

He may not have known about Oliver's plans, but it was no excuse. He should never have taken part in such a despicable act. He had been remorseful after the incident, but he could not remember who the girl was, much less make amends, and since no one knew, he decided to forget about it altogether.

Natalie had every right to go after his reputation. Hell, he deserved more than a ruined reputation for what he had, and still was, putting her and her family through.

"You are a devil, Oliver," Jasper spat, moving toward the door. He needed to find Natalie. Immediately. "I want you out of my house, and I do not ever want to set eyes upon you again. And you will do well to return every single thing you stole from the Reeves, or else—"

"You will exile me?" Oliver put in insolently.

The anger Jasper had been trying to keep at bay exploded, and in one swift movement, he had Oliver pinned on his desk and gasping for breath. "Or else I will make you wish you were never born," he corrected. "And you will also publish another paper, countering all the lies you wrote about Natalie in this one. You will formally apologize to her, too. Do I make myself clear?"

A choking Oliver nodded. Barely. Jasper dragged him out and threw him down the hallway before stepping around him and walking away. He found Wayne and asked him to ensure Oliver was out of his manor.

How would he begin apologizing to Natalie? He needed to find her as soon as possible, and he dashed out of the room.

He met Phoebe near the entrance to the ballroom, but the guests swarmed them before he could speak to her, everyone asking questions about the fight. Fresh rage gripped him.

"Be quiet!" he bellowed. "You ask me about the fight you all stood by and watched? Yet you accuse others of inaction. It was a spot of fun for you, was it not? One you would waste no time in reporting to the press."

A dead silence fell over them, and some even had the grace to look away in embarrassment.

"I will tell you this," he carried on as Phoebe's hand came onto his shoulder. "Do what you will with this story. Life means much more than jabbing fingers and looking accusingly upon innocent people. Hypocrites built this society, and I will not be a part of it any longer," he finished and turned to Phoebe, whispering, "Where is she?"

"She left with her family."

Jasper retrieved his cloak and marched to the stables. He found a mount and rode toward Clifford House.

About fifteen minutes later, it began to snow, and he lost some visibility, which forced him to slow down. Very quickly, the snowfall became so heavy that it almost completely obscured his view. Still, he pushed on. Jasper was chasing his heart, and he would walk through the pits of Hell to get to her if he had to. *Nothing* was going to stop him.

He might already be a dead man, but he refused to go before making amends with the woman he loved more than anything in existence.

A freight wagon appeared suddenly, startling his mount and sending the horse rearing. Jasper was thrown off, and he barely had time to catch the breath that had been knocked out of him before the wagon ran over him.

Pain he had never felt crushed him, and a part of the conveyance hit his head, plunging him into blindness.

He remained laying there, still, in the icy snow, as his breaths came in short and rapid releases.

Over the next moments, his bare hands felt as if they frosted, and his body grew numb, beginning from his outer limbs, with the sensation gradually thawing away to his core.

He released a final breath that soothed him into an empty darkness.

This was it. At five-and-thirty, he was meeting his ineluctable fate.

Chapter Thirty-Four

Ignominy could not describe what Natalie walked out of Amsthorne Manor with. Oliver had succeeded in soiling her family's name in society's eyes at last, but the evening bore some light in the end, because they returned home to find her father's former solicitor waiting for them.

"I had to come when I received your letter," Mr. Alcott said to George. "Lord Ecklehill has no claims over this house. The late Earl never signed any agreement. He never acted without my advice, and he would have told me about this. He also could not have given it to him because the property's entail ended the week he passed away."

Natalie held Hannah's hand tightly, feeling some hope at last.

"Thank you, Mr. Alcott," George said, his spirits elevated, too. His eye was bruised, and so was his jaw. "We received an offer for the house, and I believe it would be wise to accept it," he added.

Natalie suggested that they get down to it immediately. London felt stifling, and she wanted to escape. They could find another home soon and move away, and since George owned a small cottage that was quite habitable in Hertfordshire, they decided to travel tomorrow to stay there for a while. Although they were waiting for Hannah to make progress with Wessberg, it was not enough for them to stay. There was peace to be found in the country, even if there was none for her heart.

After Alcott's departure, Natalie decided to visit Mary and bid her farewell. She lived above her shop, and Natalie had one more dress to give her. She donned her cloak and rode the carriage to Bond Street.

"I was not expecting you," Mary said as she ushered her into the shop. She was working late with her assistant. "Especially on the night of the ball."

"Can we speak alone?" Natalie asked, and Mary led her to a room in the back. They sat by the fire, and Natalie told her all that had happened, and that they were leaving town.

Mary hugged her. "I am so sorry, Natalie…"

Mary's brother, Albert, walked into the room just then and set down a bag before taking a lantern. Natalie and Mary noticed his urgency, and his sister stopped him.

"Where are you off to in such a hurry, Albert? In this bad weather, too," Mary asked.

"The Duke of Amsthorne was run over by a wagon on the road to his manor. I was told just now and I want to go see for myself. It was ghastly, and they might need help moving him."

Natalie stopped breathing, and she felt as if her spirit had left her body and was observing the exchange between Mary and Albert.

"Some even say that the Duke is dead," he continued. "It happened near a farmhouse midway between here and the manor."

Albert is wrong, she told herself. It could not be Jasper. When Albert asked Mary not to wait for him, something awakened inside Natalie, and she bolted to her feet. "I have to see him," she said to no one. "He needs me." She looked at Albert. "Are you riding?"

"Yes."

"I am coming with you."

"But—"

"Please," she implored, tears streaming down her cheeks, and as soon as he nodded, Natalie ran out of the shop to her family's carriage, asking the driver to tell George and Hannah where she would be. Then, Albert helped her onto his horse, and they rode quickly toward Amsthorne Manor.

As their mount covered the distance, her insides knotted painfully while her nails dug into her palms. They saw a wagon moving along the road, but she thought nothing of it until she saw a figure under a pile of blankets.

"Jasper!" she called, then tapped Albert. "That is the Duke! Stop!"

She dismounted and ran to the wagon, which slowed on her approach. "I am Lady Natalie and I know this man. He needs me."

She did not wait for the man driving the wagon to answer before she climbed in and reached under the blankets for Jasper's lifeless hands.

Chapter Thirty-Five

"He needs a physician immediately, My Lady," the driver said. "I found him a while ago, and I am returning him to the manor."

"Yes. Let us go," Natalie replied. She felt some relief knowing that he was still alive, but there was a cut on his forehead that had been bound with a flimsy strip of linen. Albert rode beside them. "What happened?" she asked the driver.

Jasper was so pale, and she had to put a hand under his nose to ensure he was breathing. He was, but barely.

"Someone ran him over, then left him. I found him and took him into my house to warm him but I think some of his bones are broken, and the cut on his head does not look good. I wanted to wait until the snow subsided before setting out but I reckon he needs a physician."

She rearranged the blankets around him before pulling the hood of her cloak over her face. The snowfall was heavier here than in town, and knowing that Jasper had been out here for a while made her more fearful. Her grip of his hand tightened, and she tried not to think as they journeyed.

Most of the guests had left when they arrived, but there were a handful of carriages in front of the manor. She jumped down from the wagon and ran to the front door, slamming the brass knocker against the wood. As soon as the butler opened, she told him that Jasper needed help, and within seconds, the butler and several footmen rushed out to carry him into the house.

"Be careful with him," she said before going to seek out Phoebe.

She found Phoebe in one of the drawing rooms with a guest. "Natalie—"

"Jasper is hurt!" she blurted, and Phoebe blanched. "He needs help."

"I-I will send for the physician," his aunt managed as Smith appeared.

"I have sent for him," he said, and Natalie and Phoebe hurried up to Jasper's chambers to be with him before the physician arrived. They sat helplessly in his sitting room as Wayne and Smith made him comfortable and warm in the bedchamber.

The physician arrived shortly, and after two hours that felt like an eternity, he met an anxious Natalie and Phoebe, wearing a grim expression.

"The Duke suffered a concussion, a broken arm, along with several ribs," he informed them. "I have done my best. He needs to rest, and we should pray to God so that His mercy may see him through this."

"Oh, my!" Phoebe choked out, collapsing onto Natalie. She held her tightly, struggling with her tears, and tried to reassure her. Now was not the time for them to crumble. They needed to stay strong for Jasper, especially Natalie. He had to wake up for her.

George and Hannah arrived and they all sat in Jasper's sitting room while he fought for his life. Natalie refused to allow herself to think of the curse he had told her about. It was too much.

The night was a brutally long one with no signs of light, and it was almost sunrise when Natalie encouraged Hannah and George to return home while she decided to stay. They were no longer traveling, and she was going to stay in the manor until he recovered.

A full forty-eight hours passed, and Jasper remained unconscious, but not unchanged, for a violent fever gripped him. The doctor came to see him, as usual, but there was little he could do.

"I am sorry. I truly am," he said. "I wish there was more I could do."

Natalie collapsed into a chair after the doctor's departure, endeavoring to be as brave as she could, but her traitorous tears came pouring forth. *I should not cry,* she reminded herself to no avail.

She had done nothing to deserve the pain she was feeling, but she had to hope. It was all that she could hold onto. Phoebe wrapped an arm around her shoulders to console her.

At least we have each other in the darkness, an encouraging voice in her mind said; though all Natalie wanted was Jasper. He was her heart, and she could not bear the thought of a world without him in it.

She sat by his bed with a damp cloth she used to cool his brow and mop his sweat. The physician had stitched his wound, and he had advised them to keep it dry and clean under the bandage. She would gently touch his face while she spoke to him. Natalie told him stories from distant shores, where there was light and laughter. It helped her breaking heart and occupied her thoughts.

Phoebe returned to the room after resting, and she encouraged Natalie to rest, too.

"You have also hardly eaten, Natalie," she said. She was right, and Natalie reluctantly relinquished her spot by Jasper's side, as Phoebe replaced her.

"What is this?" she heard her say as she made for the door. Stopping, she turned to see Phoebe removing a black mask from Jasper's nightstand drawer. "I thought I would find a book here but certainly not this. Is it a mask?"

Phoebe studied it carefully, her fingers trailing over the lacey fabric. Natalie wanted to tell her that it was perhaps nothing, but Phoebe turned it around, as if inspecting some precious gem.

"It looks awfully a lot like the Rogue's mask," she noted. "Natalie, does it not?"

Natalie bit her bottom lip, wishing to tell her it was a mere coincidence, or that perhaps someone dropped it there. It would sound silly.

"Uh...I'm unsure," was all she said.

"Oh, but it is. Look, it has the same markings." Phoebe continued her monologue and her inspection, and Natalie held her breath as she was unsure if she should reveal Jasper's secret or not. Would he have wanted it? It would be best if he told her himself.

"Do you know anything of this, Natalie?"

"I...uh---"

"Oh, speak child, I am certainly not that naïve," Phoebe said, placing the mask on the bed. "Staying late outside, returning with headaches, acting strange and aloof. All so unlike my Jasper. Tell me, is he truly the Rogue? My Jasper?"

Natalie's muscles stiffened, and she turned to stare at Phoebe's pleading eyes, regretting it. The poor woman was worried sick and only needed an answer for her nephew's odd behavior.

Natalie nodded silently.

"Oh, dear!" Phoebe's hands traveled to her lips in surprise. "All this while, I never knew. I never connected the dots, how foolish of me." She tapped the mask, then returned to Natalie once more. "What about the Comtesse? What do you know of her?"

Natalie held her breath, her cheeks—no, her whole body reddening and heating from embarrassment. Oh goodness, having to explain that she was, in fact, the Comtesse should not be as embarrassing as it felt. But she couldn't help herself. Her mouth opened and closed like a fish struggling to breathe out of water and Phoebe's eyes widened just then.

"Oh, my!" Phoebe exclaimed. "You, my dear, have a lot of explaining to do." It was half a command, half teasing, as a smile played against her lips.

"And you, gentleman," Phoebe turned to her nephew. "You best hurry and wake up, for you have a lot of answering to do." Fresh tears welled in her eyes and Natalie held her hand in comfort.

The next day looked promising. Jasper's fever subsided, but he lay absolutely still with his face very pale. Natalie continued to tell him stories, not sure he could hear her.

Her cousins spent their days in the manor, and Natalie's clothes had been brought over the day after Jasper's accident. The entire town was aware of what had occurred, and Mary had visited twice.

Sometime in the early hours of the morning, Natalie's exhausted mind and body took the reins from her pain and forced her to sleep. It was a fitful slumber, one filled with longing for Jasper's recovery. She awoke with a start when she felt a hand on hers.

She looked up, expecting to see Phoebe, but instead met Jasper's blue gaze, and it was his hand touching hers.

"Jasper!" she cried, blinking. "Oh my God, you are awake!" Natalie was crying, and she did not bother to hide it.

Phoebe ran into the room right then, and when she made to throw herself at him, Natalie reminded her of his injuries. The physician was sent for immediately. Jasper did not speak, and it was evident that he was in pain. But he was awake! He was going to live!

"It is a miracle!" the physician declared after examining him. "The fevers were most concerning, but now that he is awake, I am certain that he will make a full recovery."

Jasper fell asleep again after being given some medicine and soup, while Phoebe went down to receive a caller. Natalie was reading when she heard him move. "Jasper," she whispered, touching his hand.

Slowly, his eyes opened, and she was certain that he was looking at her. They had been blank and unfocused before.

"I..." His voice was hoarse and raspy.

"Do not speak until you are better."

He shook his head very slightly and winced, likely from the pain the movement caused. "Natalie, my love," he whispered, and her eyes instantly filled with tears.

"Jasper, please," she said in a low voice. "You mustn't talk." Oh, but she wished to hear his every word.

"I need...to tell you this," he said. "I...I needed to find you. To apologize for...everything."

She moved to sit beside him on the bed, stroking his stubbled jaw. He reached his arm up, cupping her cheek. "...I hurt you, years ago. And I...I had no idea. Christ, I did not know, my love."

He coughed, and she instinctively reached closer to him. "I forgive you, but please don't tire yourself. You need rest."

Ignoring her, he continued. "I hurt you so bad, Natalie. I ruined you and I—Bloody hell, I love you. I love you so much Natalie, my heart feels like it will break."

"I forgave you the day I fell in love with you." When his eyebrows rose, she smiled. "Yes, Jasper. I love you too."

He took her hand and raised it to his lips. He could not hold her, but Natalie knew how much he wished to. "I love you more than anything in this world." His eyes misted. "I feared losing you more than I feared my death."

She kissed his cheeks, then his lips. He continued after a slight but painful groan, "I did not know about Oliver, or what he did. But...But if I knew, I swear I would have protected you." He coughed as he tried to raise himself, but Natalie held him down, making him stay reclined. "I would have killed him if that's what it would take to keep you safe and happy. I was young and foolish, but that is not an excuse. I never intended to hurt you and I'll have to live with that for the rest of my life—I'll need to make it up to you for the rest of my life."

"All I want is for you to recover. Whatever happened was not your fault and I've forgiven you a long time ago. Everything else will be taken care of." She kissed him again, brushing the tears that rolled down his cheeks. All was well. He was alive, and he was hers. Her wish to be wanted and loved had come true. And so had her final item on the list.

Epilogue

Three months later

The Duke of Amsthorne has recovered as we hoped he would. We have news from a very reliable source that he is in love with Lady Natalie Reeves. Our heads are tilted to catch the sound of wedding bells from Westminster Abbey. By turning our attention to the Duke and Lady Natalie, we are not abandoning our search and speculation about the Masked Rogue of London and his Comtesse De Villepin. We simply have no wish to continue upon an unyielding path.

M*y love,*
Smith will retrieve you at two o'clock. There is something beautiful that I wish to show you.

J.

. . .

Natalie folded the note and grinned at Hannah. "It is from Jasper."

Hannah jumped, then lowered her voice. "Are you meeting Jasper or the Rogue tonight?"

"Not night, two o'clock," Natalie corrected, glancing at the clock. Her eyes widened. "I have to get dressed now or I shall be late!"

Hannah grew alarmed, too, when she saw the time. "An hour is hardly enough for a lady to dress. What do you want to wear?" She ran to Natalie's wardrobe.

"The dark green satin," Natalie replied, undoing her hair, then the buttons of her dress. She had seen him the day before but she felt tiny flutters everywhere at the thought of seeing him again.

With Hannah's help, she dressed in time to meet Smith. This time, she did not sneak out of the house through the servants' entrance, but instead walked out the front door to the waiting carriage. She did not know where they were going, but she sat and looked out the window, wringing a lace handkerchief in anticipation.

An hour later, the carriage rolled to a halt and she was helped down. Looking about, she realized they were at the docks. Natalie was led aboard a ship, and standing on the deck was Jasper, looking impossibly handsome in a dark blue velvet tailcoat, and a gray waistcoat. His wounds had healed very well, and he was almost himself again.

"You are late, Lady Natalie," he teased, and a wide grin spread across her face.

"I ought to give you a strong word for sending the note very late. I only had an hour to prepare."

"Forgive me, my love. Aunt Phoebe insisted I saw the physician the instant I sat to write to you."

Natalie's eyes moved over him. "How are you?"

"Strong as a horse." He grinned and took her hands, raising them to his lips in turn. "Shall we?"

"Whatever are we doing on a ship, Jasper?" she asked as he led her toward the bow of the magnificent vessel.

"You will see." He winked, and she saw that they were preparing to leave the docks.

"Who owns this ship?"

"I do," he answered with a small measure of self-satisfaction.

Natalie feigned indifference when she saw his smugness increase.

He laughed. "You are supposed to be impressed, Natalie. Can you not tell that I am desperately attempting to do so?" They stopped near the bow, and he tenderly stroked her cheek.

"Very well, I am impressed." She looked around. "I am also curious about where we are going."

"China," he said, and she blinked.

"You are in jest."

He did not look as though he was, but then he laughed. "We are only going out to the sea for a few hours. As I said, I have something beautiful to show you."

"I do not mind traveling to China," she murmured happily, turning to look at the sun painting the sky ethereally with orange and pink.

"Natalie, my love," he said, and she faced him. His expression made her heart race.

"Yes?"

"An angel came to me while I slept, and she told me of adventures on distant shores." Jasper pulled the lace glove on her left hand and kissed her fingers. Natalie's eyes widened in surprise. Her stories... He had heard them, after all. "What say you, we chase our story on those tides? Marry me, Natalie. Let us write every chapter together." His eyes were full of hope and love.

His fear was gone, and so had hers. "Yes, Jasper. I will marry you!"

He wrapped his arms around her and kissed her deeply. "I love you, Natalie."

"And I love you."

The End?

Extended Epilogue

Six years later

Today marks the twelfth year of the Rogue. London, we know that without this man, life would be utterly dull. Although we are still curious, we no longer wish to unmask him. The great service he does society is enough. However, we would like to see him more often. Once or twice a year is ridiculous! How can we persuade our dear Masked Rogue to make merry on our streets more? What more can we do to prove that we deserve his presence?
Then there is our Comtesse, who is more elusive than the Rogue. It has been over a year, but every woman wishes to be her. It is no longer a secret that she is married to the Masked Rogue but there are many unfortunate men who still dream of attaining her.

"London wishes to know what color and style the Comtesse would wear next time she is out in town," Phoebe declared as she set aside the gossip sheet she had been reading.

Once in a while, the Rogue and Comtesse went out to play, giving the aristocracy a little treat to treasure until the next time. Society's obsession with them had only grown, and the ladies were beginning to match their fashion to the Comtesse's, but with a few *modest* changes.

EXTENDED EPILOGUE

"Oh, that is nonsense!" Hannah said from her seat. She was happily married to Wessberg, and she had just told Natalie that morning that she was carrying her second child. She no longer wrote for The Londoner, claiming it was because of their obsession with the Rogue and Comtesse.

Natalie knew the actual reason was that she had enjoyed the quest for their identity, and once she knew, she lost all interest. Besides, her five-year-old daughter, Rosalie, kept Hannah occupied.

"If ladies of the *ton* truly wish to be inspired by the Comtesse's style," Hannah continued, "then they should not change anything about it."

"How scandalous that would be!" Phoebe laughed.

"Society would never do that, Hannah," Natalie giggled.

"Oh, but it is certain to add a very interesting twist to things, do you not agree?" Phoebe said with a sly glint in her eyes.

Before Natalie could respond, her son's beleaguered nurse, Miss Davis, walked into the drawing room.

"I cannot find him, Your Grace," she said. "I have looked everywhere!"

"Oh, dear." Natalie set down her teacup and got to her feet, walking out of the room. She asked the nurse to search the upper floors again while Natalie would look around the first floor.

She had just rounded a corner in the hallway when something poked one of her legs from behind. "En garde!" came a tiny but familiar voice.

Natalie smiled before she turned to the sight of her five-year-old son, Henry. He was clutching a small foil, and his large blue eyes were sparkling. He looked just like Jasper, but instead of raven hair, his was a tawny color that she thought was utterly adorable.

"Well done, Henry," Natalie chuckled. "What a clever way to run from Miss Davis."

"I run from her because she refuses to fence with me," he complained.

EXTENDED EPILOGUE

"*I* will play with you soon," she reassured him as her eyes moved around for his companion. "Where is Rosalie?" They ought to be together, and Natalie felt a little nervous about what mischief the girl would get up to by herself.

"I do not know," Henry replied, but there was a glint in his eyes that said otherwise.

"Very well, then. Since you have lost your cousin, I suppose we could not be fencing anytime soon," Natalie said and waited patiently for his reaction. His eyes darted to the side as he contemplated.

"I know where she is, Mama." He led Natalie up to the room she used as a workroom, and sitting atop a pile of fabrics was Rosalie. She had silk and lace sashes draped all over her, and she hummed a cheerful tune, unaware of their presence. Henry covered his mouth to keep from laughing.

Now that she was a duchess without any financial troubles, she no longer needed to sew, but she occasionally made dresses for herself in the style she preferred, and of course, for the Comtesse De Villepin.

Natalie cleared her throat, and Rosalie started, turning and giving her a sheepish look. "Aunt Natalie, I was..." she trailed off and looked away.

Natalie smiled and offered the girl her hand. "Come, I have some sugar plums for you." Taking Rosalie and Henry's hands, she returned them to the drawing room.

Her heart fluttered the instant they walked in and she saw Jasper, who had just returned from the House of Lords.

"En garde!" Henry jumped forward with his flimsy foil, challenging his father.

Natalie watched with so much warmth in her heart as her husband sparred with their son with an invisible saber.

"I concede!" Henry cried when their sparring ended in his defeat, and Jasper scooped him up, tickling him.

EXTENDED EPILOGUE

Miss Davis appeared just as Jasper set him down and Henry let out a squeal in protest before running to hide behind Phoebe. It was time for his violin lessons, and although he was developing his talent, it would appear he did not wish to attend today. Phoebe picked a shortbread from the tea tray, and after much placation, she got him to acquiesce.

❦

"I hope you will come to Kent to celebrate Michaelmas with us. Yours always, George." Jasper looked up at Natalie from the missive he had just finished reading and smiled.

George was inviting them to the country where he was happily rusticating with his wife and two children. The Clifford fortunes had recovered. In fact, Jasper had invested greatly in the Coal Factory and Mines after it was taken away from Oliver, and the business was thriving, now more than ever.

As for Oliver, he left England, and no one knew where he was. Not that any of them cared. He had caused them so much pain that they wanted no news of him. There was a rumor about him losing all of his wealth, however.

"So, Comtesse." Jasper set the missive down. "What color is it going to be next?" he asked the question that London desperately sought an answer to. He was still impressed by his wife's skill, and how she made daring dresses for the Comtesse. Dresses that drove him mad with lust.

"I was thinking of violet," Natalie replied as he pulled her close and trailed kisses down her jawline. They had made it a habit over the years where he was not allowed to see the Comtesse's dresses until she wore them on the nights they played.

"Violet..." Jasper mused. "Then I might have the perfect thing to go with it." He reached into the nightstand drawer and pulled out a small box, handing it to her.

Her brilliant eyes sparkled like ambers, and when she opened the box, a little gasp escaped her. Sitting on a velvet cushion was a tear-shaped amethyst ring, surrounded by tiny diamonds. Natalie stared at the gift in awe, and he removed it from the box and slipped it onto her slender finger.

"This is lovely, Jasper!" she breathed. "The Comtesse is the amethyst, and the diamonds her admirers," she said, and he began to laugh. Her eyes met his. "Do you think we should name our second child Amethyst? If a girl, of course."

"That is an excellent name." He kissed her fingers. "Did you know that the Amethyst symbolizes healing?" he murmured.

"It does?"

"Yes. My broken soul found salvation when you walked into my life, Natalie." He cradled her cheeks and placed a soft kiss on her forehead. "Thank you for healing me, and for teaching my heart how to love and hope again."

"Oh, Jasper." She did not need to say anything because he could see every emotion in her eyes. He kissed her lips for several seconds, reveling in her familiar yet sensually intoxicating taste.

Her brows creased in thought when he pulled away, and she suddenly asked, "How did you know to get a ring that would fit the Comtesse's next dress?"

"I was thinking of what ring to get you, and Rosalie happened to reveal to me that she saw a beautiful violet dress in your workroom. It gave me the notion to, and when I discovered what the gem symbolizes, it was all I needed to proceed."

She wrapped her arms around his neck and climbed onto his lap. He hardened immediately, and his arms moved to circle her waist. His mouth was seeking the soft skin of her neck when a thought came to him.

"What do you think of the Rogue and his Comtesse paying London a visit tonight?" he asked, watching her eyes grow wide with surprise and anticipation. Their visits were sporadic, and they often dressed as their alter egos to please each other.

Making an unexpected appearance tonight was bound to shake society, and luckily, his wife was just as much of a rogue. She climbed out of the bed and ran to the dressing room. When she reappeared, she was holding a daring violet silk dress.

Jasper rose to help her dress, glancing at the clock and calculating how long that would take. It was past eleven, and if he behaved himself, she would be ready in fifteen minutes.

An hour later, he offered Natalie his hand. He had promised to behave but she had been too tempting to resist, and he had to give her pleasure. "Are you ready?"

"I am ready for anything, Jasper, with you by my side." She gave him a brilliant smile.

"And you shall always have me, my love." He stole a kiss before they disappeared into the night, as the Rogue and his Comtesse that they were, and always would be.

The End.

PREVIEW: TO RUIN A DUKE

Turn the page for a sweet preview of:

Chapter One

Frederick pushed his mount to a canter. The woodland flowed by in a series of sun-blessed greens. The path was wide here and well-worn from the long grass that grew beneath the trees. For a moment he allowed himself the simple pleasure of enjoying the breeze that kissed his face.

How long since I did nothing except ride? And when I have ridden, how long has it been since that ride was for no purpose other than enjoying the countryside?

The answer was *too long*. Too long spent administering the business of his estates. Too long spent amid his easels and paints.

A man should take some time for himself.

The woods petered out at the brow of a hill. Before him stretched the countryside of East Sussex. He was looking south, towards the distant coast. Somewhere to his left would be Pevensey Bay, further left still, along the coast would be Hastings and his own estate of Valhurst. He reined the horse in and sat for a moment, looking out over the quiet, checkered landscape of fields, meadows, and woods, taking a deep breath of air.

His thoughts strayed to the work that needed to be done at Valhurst. The urge to paint, to produce something of value. Recreation was not something Frederick found easy. He sighed.

That is the burden of a Dukedom. To be a good Duke, one must give oneself to the people and the land. I am a conservator, just as my father taught me. Even the art is something of an indulgence.

Something caught his eye, moving quickly across a meadow below. He shaded the sun from his eyes and realized that he was looking at a woman riding. Oddly, she seemed to be riding astride her mount, not side-saddle as women were supposed to. As he watched, the animal leaped an obstacle and the woman let out a whoop. Dark brown hair streamed behind her and she seemed to be wearing breeches.

Upon my soul. I do believe that is exactly what she's wearing. Not a dress but a man's attire. Now there's a hell of a thing.

Intrigued, he nudged his mount to a walk, calculating a route that appeared to intercept the woman's path. She was riding up a slope now towards him. Frederick came to a stone wall, bordering the field at its highest point. He followed it to a three-bar wooden gate, weather-marked and aged. He waited there as the woman angled her steed for the same spot. As she reached the gate, he dismounted and untied the thick rope that had been used to hold the gate shut.

"Good afternoon!" the woman said, red-cheeked and bright-eyed. "And thank you."

She had a tumble of dark hair, flowing loosely to her shoulders in bouncing curls. Her eyes were hazel. Frederick noted a stray leaf wedged between the buttons of her coat, another in the curls of her hair. A smudge of bark or moss adhered to a freckled cheek just beneath her left eye.

"You are welcome, madame," Frederick said. "And a good afternoon to you too. That was a fine jump."

"Oh, that was all Hettie here." The woman smiled, patting her horse's neck. "We came to a ditch and Hettie decided she could clear it."

"And clearly outran your companions," Frederick said as he closed and retied the gate, the woman having ridden through.

"What companions?" she said.

"You are surely not out riding alone?" Frederick asked, genuinely surprised.

"I surely am, though I am returning home if that makes you feel better."

It was said with a mischievous smile that Frederick found himself returning. It was impossible not to.

"Do you disapprove?" she asked.

"It is not for me to approve or disapprove of your actions," Frederick said. "I think merely of the safety of a young woman, riding alone in the middle of the countryside."

"This is Sussex," the woman replied with a grin. "How dangerous can it be?"

Frederick did not like the casual attitude.

Doesn't she know there could be brigands, former soldiers, or other vagrants on these roads? Perhaps she genuinely does not. If so, it is my duty to be her escort.

"For you, any potential danger is magnified because of your sex. May I ask where home is?"

"Perhaps I should not say, as you are a stranger and as you have just been warning me of the perils for a lone female."

There was a playful smile on the young woman's face which told Frederick that she wasn't taking him seriously. He returned the smile thinly, gritting his teeth but hiding the fact behind closed lips.

"Quite right. I am Frederick Smith, Thirteenth Duke of Valhurst. That is some dozen miles or so to the east of here. And yourself?"

She didn't answer but instead sat her horse, gazing out over the spread of countryside before them. She was quite exquisitely pretty, with round cheeks that held a rosy hue and eyes that seemed to sparkle. Rosebud lips seemed to adopt a smile as their natural expression. Frederick looked away when he caught himself staring. The breeches she wore ended at tall riding boots which showed a well-shaped calf. Her garments were quite scandalous, showing off the shape of her legs.

"I came from all the way over there. Do you see the woods on the horizon at the foot of that hill? Came across country and at one point was chased by a man I believe mistook me for a poacher."

She laughed but Frederick was shocked.

"It was quite the chase for a time. I was forced to cut right across country."

"Did he catch you? Is that why you look so…"

He tailed off realizing there was no polite way of finishing the sentence. But he was genuinely concerned. Game keepers could be brutal to those they believed were intending to poach.

"Like I've been dragged through a hedge backward?" the woman laughed. "No, he did not catch me. But, yes, the chase is the reason. Ah well, one does not ride in the country and expect to look ready for a ball. More like a bath!"

"That is why England possesses roads, madame," Frederick said. "So that gentlemen and women do not need to appear disheveled. You are lucky to have escaped, nonetheless."

"Not luck, Your Grace. I was the better horseman, horsewoman I should say."

In Frederick's experience, that was an unusual thing. He did not know any woman who would not take a carriage rather than a horse. Men were far more common as riders than women and even then, women rode side-saddle to accommodate their clothing, a significant hindrance.

"I note you do not ride side-saddle. That will have helped you to outrun a man on horseback, certainly."

"It helps, but I can beat any horsemen, even riding side-saddle as convention dictates I should."

Her manner was almost confrontational, the sting taken out by her impish smile.

A very direct young lady indeed.

Frederick found himself warming to her. She was remarkably different from any woman of his association in the past. Certainly different to the women making up the Ton, who formed Frederick's primary society.

Refreshingly different. Though reckless in the extreme.

"You do not believe me, Your Grace?" she asked.

"That you could out-ride a skilled horseman while riding side-saddle? No, frankly I do not," Frederick said.

"Very well. Let us put it to the test. I propose a race. Through these woods to the Longbridge road on the other side. That is about a mile or so, I believe."

Frederick had to stop himself from gaping. The young woman promptly swung a leg up and over the cantle of her saddle so that she was sitting side-saddle. The glimpse that briefly gave Frederick of her legs in a position that no man other than a husband should be allowed to see, took his breath away. He composed himself.

"I will not take advantage," he demurred.

"Meaning you consider me to be boastful and foolish?" the woman challenged.

"Far from it. Mistaken is all," Frederick replied.

"You're on. Keep up, Your Grace, if you can."

She flicked the reins and clicked her tongue. The horse responded immediately, taking a couple of steps before accelerating into a canter. Frederick whirled his own mount and dug in his heels. The horse leaped to a gallop and, after a quick look over her shoulder, the young woman urged her own steed to the same speed. The race was on.

Chapter Two

※

Jane looked back over her shoulder to see the handsome young Duke spurring his horse to follow her. On seeing him at the gate, his beauty had quite taken her breath away. Broad shoulders with black hair and shocking blue eyes.

The eyes of a hunter, sharp and alert. How thrilling!

Flustered by those piercing eyes, Jane had resorted to her usual defense, a cheeky disregard for convention and an irresistible urge to poke fun at pomposity.

Not that he seems entirely pompous. But any man who indulges in a ride through the countryside as well-attired as this man thinks altogether too highly of himself.

Jane had dressed herself in a coat reserved for the outdoors and a light blue and white dress that was not one of her best. And the only reason for that concession was that the lecture she would receive from Cousin Ernest, if she dirtied a good dress, would be more than she could bear.

There will be enough of a lecture as it is. I surely will not be able to get home from here for at least three hours. That means I will be late for dinner. Aunt

Louisa will laugh if I tell her I was delayed while I raced a Duke. Ernest will have apoplexy. Botheration!

The blue-eyed Duke was gaining on her. But she had not been bragging. To ride side-saddle at speed took exceptional balance and a strong relationship with the horse. Hettie responded to the reins as instinctively as most mounts did for the pressure of their rider's knees. She also understood a range of voice commands.

I will show the pompous Duke how gender does not have a bearing on horsemanship.

The sound of thundering hooves was growing loud in her ears. Another glance back showed the Duke less than a horse-length behind her. He was standing in the saddle, revealing shapely legs. His face was set. It was strong with a firm jaw and flat planes of cheeks and slightly tilted cheekbones. There was something exotic in those features that spoke of origins beyond England.

Maybe he is descended from a gypsy prince. A King of the Romany. Or a rebellious Welsh prince.

A branch snatched at her hair, whipping past her as she veered too close to the trees that crowded to either side of the path. Jane shrieked at the sudden touch, more invigoration than genuine fear.

Time to concentrate, Jane Grant. My goodness, I did not even return the Duke the courtesy of my name. How rude he must think of me. Botheration!

Jane hunched forward as more limber branches slashed by. The Duke was close enough that Jane could hear the snorting breath of his horse. Its nose was level with Hettie's croup now.

So, he is faster in a straight race. But how good is he in a steeplechase?

Seeing an opening in the trees to her left, Jane steered Hettie through it with a tug of the reins. The Duke almost missed the turn, but managed to stay with her. Jane grinned to herself, focusing her concentration on the terrain ahead. A small clearing had been formed by a fallen tree. Hettie leaped the log without breaking stride or balking.

Jane instinctively shifted her position to brace for the landing. Then they were among the trees. Jane sought out a path between maples and birch. Here, Hettie's nimble feet and her rider's skill began to make the difference.

A quick look back over her shoulder was risked and Jane saw the gap widening.

Not doing so well when you can't predict the path, handsome Duke.

His face was now a mask of determination, set as though from stone. Blue eyes were fixed on her and Jane resisted the urge to stick out her tongue.

That would be going too far. I must maintain some decorum or even Aunt Louisa will have words for me. But, by God, this is fun!

Hettie was beginning to tire, Jane could tell. If her sturdy mount was flagging, then her pursuer must also be tired. Jane looked back once more to see that the Duke was almost out of sight. Across the uneven and unpredictable terrain of the deep woods, he had been unable to keep up with her. For herself, these woods were not as familiar as the Ashdown Forest which had been her playground since she could walk, but still, those childhood experiences had stood her in good stead.

Seeing a dip in the land ahead, she steered Hettie into it and, when she thought she must be lost to the sight of the Duke, doubled back. She ensured that thick undergrowth was kept between her and her opponent in this steeplechase, walking Hettie until she heard him thundering by, screened from her by a tangle of hawthorn and briars. Smiling to herself, she let Hettie find her own pace, confident that the Duke had lost her in the woods.

What a lovely day it has been. A visit to see Mary Jones' new baby over at Cookham Farm, then a pleasant ramble across the country to work up an appetite.

Ernest's dour, disapproving face loomed in her mind and she sighed. She wished that her circumstances were such that she could ignore Cousin Ernest and his disapproval. She wished to be free, as her parents had been, unshackled by the expectations of society. Louisa, the Dowager Marchioness and Ernest's mother, was free, caring little for the opinions of her peers and indulging in her passion for the arts. But, the house belonged to Ernest. He was Earl and, while Louisa was protected by the fact that he was her son, Jane's familial connection was weaker.

And so I must bow my head and look contrite when Ernest summons me to his study like a wayward child. It is all very well for Aunt Louisa to keep company with artists, poets, and actors. He can't control her, so doubles his efforts to control me.

She had left the house in a respectable dress, changing at Cookham into the more practical breeches and boots that she now wore.

It would serve Ernest right if I marched into Welterham in my breeches and boots. See how he likes that.

It would not happen, however. Jane could not provoke him too much. Not until she had contrived a way that she might live on her own, out from under Ernest's thumb. The living left to her by her father was insufficient to rent a house of her own, however. She tried to put her circumstances from her mind.

I do not know what the future will bring or when Ernest will next allow me to spend the day out on my own like this. I must not waste a minute in a brown study.

Her thoughts returned to the pompous, but handsome, Duke. Jane glanced over her shoulder as though he might be there following. Part of her hoped he would be, though she knew he was left a long way behind.

And undoubtedly is no tracker. Not a man who goes riding in a silk waistcoat and a fine royal blue coat. Mary Jones and her husband could live for a year on the cost of that wardrobe.

But such an interesting face. Austere, as was his manner to a degree. Strong and unyielding in a way that inspired attraction but also a thrill of fear.

The face of a barbarian raider. Had he caught me, he is probably strong enough to do with me as he wishes.

The thought sent a tingle of excitement through her and a flush of color to her cheeks. Jane smiled to herself and shook her head at the wanton thoughts. If ever she saw him again, she would be scarlet. Still, it was not as though she would ever see him again, so that was a remote risk. Ahead, the woodland was becoming sparse and long grass swayed in the gentle breeze between slender boles. A few sheep were munching their way through it, some looked up as Hettie walked by but most ignored her.

Jane looked out to the horizon. Somewhere beyond that lay the English Channel. Beyond that was France and then, if you kept on, the Mediterranean and Africa.

Papa has traveled that road, to Africa and beyond even that. I wonder if I will ever get to tread in his footsteps. See Cairo, or Madrid perhaps. And what of Delhi and Calcutta? One day, Jane, one day.

Chapter Three

Fiery gold still clung to the western sky when Frederick arrived within sight of Valhurst Abbey. The sunset was behind him, while ahead, purple shaded to black and the first stars were becoming visible in a cloudless sky. The road wound around an outcrop of woods and then through the tall, white gateposts that marked the entrance to Valhurst's park. From there it crossed the open expanse of long grass, dotted with trees, and roamed by deer. Once it had been the fields of the abbey that the house had once been. Now it was purely ornamental, a setting for the jewel that was the house itself.

Valhurst stood dark against the deeper dark of the night sky. It rambled, stretching out its wings in seemingly random directions, the product of past Dukes deciding to build and extend without any real thought of future need. It had two ruined towers, their tops unfinished and jagged, crenelated rooftops and brick walls that stood cheek by jowl with the stone blocks and primitive mortar of the middle ages.

He was proud of his home. It was a testament to the durability of the English aristocracy and a symbol of his main duty, to preserve these lands for future generations.

A duty I have neglected today. For what purpose? Recreation and a frankly reckless race through the woods after a rather wild young woman. Utter foolishness.

Frederick kicked his horse to a trot, wanting to be home as quickly as possible to make up for the time he had lost. The sight of the ruined north and south towers irked him, as they always did. It was an imperfection that he longed to either rebuild or demolish entirely. The house was hardly symmetrical anyway but it could be brought more into order. Except that would go against the duty, solemnly inherited from his father, to preserve and protect. At least the grounds and gardens were ordered. A veritable army of groundskeepers was employed to ensure that Valhurst Abbey was famous throughout England for its neat, ordered, and controlled gardens.

After handing the reins of his mount to a stable hand, he hurried inside. A servant took his coat, folding it carefully over one arm. Frederick paused, picking a stray piece of lint from the man's lapel, then holding it up so the servant could see it. No words were necessary. A gloved hand took the lint and pocketed it. Frederick cast a cursory glance over the man's uniform, then nodded.

I shall have to speak to Hawley about that. The household should be paying close attention to detail when it comes to their attire.

The hall was of stone and lit by chandeliers high above, hanging from an impressively arched roof. Framed paintings by acknowledged masters hung in neat lines that led the eye to a central staircase, broken only by the doors leading to the ballroom on one side and a reception room, drawing room and library on the other.

"Lord Ashwick arrived thirty-three minutes ago, Your Grace," the servant informed him. "He awaits you in the Garden Library."

The Garden Library was the name given to the public room overlooking a walled garden on the west side of the house. Frederick's own private study and library, known as the Abbot's Library, was upstairs forming part of his personal suite. Frederick took out a gold and silver chased pocket watch, flipped the cover open, and regarded the face for a moment.

"He is twelve minutes late, I see. Very well. Dismissed."

The servant bowed and turned to walk away while Frederick headed for the third door on the right of the hall. Opening it, he saw a young man with fiery red-gold hair, standing before the fire with a clay pipe in one hand. He was looking at a watercolor above the mantle.

"This one of yours Freddie?" he asked.

"It is one of mine, Edmund. Do you like it?" Frederick said, closing the door behind him.

A decanter of brandy stood on a polished table beside an armchair. Edmund had poured two drinks. Frederick took one, inhaling appreciatively over it.

"How you can smoke that thing I do not understand. You look like a farm hand," Frederick said.

"A relic from my past. I found it easier to carry a pipe like this when I was on campaign than a humidor of cigars. Frightfully inconvenient on the battlefield, eh?" Edmund grinned around his battered and scratched pipe.

"I wouldn't know old chap."

"And in answer to your question. I haven't the foggiest notion. Paint is paint. I can't tell good from bad. Knowing you though, I am sure it is excellent," Edmund replied.

"It is passable," Frederick said modestly. "By the way, I must apologize for not being here to greet you. I fully expected to be but was delayed."

"I hadn't even thought about it, old man," Edmund said breezily.

An entirely true statement too. Edmund does not pay much mind to punctuality.

"What delayed you?" Edmund asked. "Any bother?"

He took one of the armchairs, collecting his brandy on the way and practically flopping into the chair, putting a booted foot casually onto a footrest. Frederick tried not to wince at the sight of shod feet on furniture, making a mental note to ensure the maids were aware.

"A waste of time. I should have been here, not gallivanting about the countryside," Frederick grumbled as he took his own seat, sipping from his brandy before replacing it on the table precisely where it had been.

"Gallivanting? You? Pray tell, this is a new development," Edmund said teasingly.

Frederick grimaced. "I decided to take a ride. I have estate ledgers to check and correspondence to catch up on, not to mention an unfinished landscape. But, I decided to indulge..."

"Hear hear," Edmund interrupted, raising his glass in toast.

"The peculiar event that delayed me though was a young woman I encountered. She was out somewhere above Pevensey, entirely on her own, riding across country and looking like she had just climbed out of a haystack!"

Edmund leaned forward with interest. "That is more the sort of adventure I find myself having, old chap. What happened?"

"Hardly an adventure. I stopped to talk to her, I felt it my duty to point out that it simply isn't safe for a young lady to roam the countryside alone. She did not heed my advice however and actually challenged me to a race if you can believe it!"

"A race!" Edmund exclaimed. "By Jove. And did you accept the challenge? More importantly, speaking as a sportsman, did you win?"

"I did not. She was quite magnificent..." Frederick looked up and saw the gleam in his friend's eye. "That is to say she was a fine horsewoman. I would have won had we stuck to the path but she veered off into the trees and it began a steeplechase. She vanished like a ghost."

Edmund chortled. "I'd like to meet this spirit of the woods. Sounds like quite the girl. What's her name?"

"That's the damnable thing. She never gave me her name. Had the appearance of a well-bred young woman from her voice. Sussex native from the accent. Certainly not a commoner I would say. But, no name given."

"A rebel against social conformity too. I'm in love," Edmund said, taking a healthy swallow of brandy.

"Really, Edmund. Be serious. It's all very modern for a young woman to be independent but hardly practical to be so…so…"

"Free?" Edmund arched an eyebrow.

"Wild," Frederick finished. "Order is important. For the gentry more than anyone. Where would the country be if we all said hang the rules and did whatever we pleased?"

"Entertaining," Edmund said after a moment's thought.

"You're impossible," Frederick replied, though not without a wry smile. "Well, it was a diversion anyway. I shall never set eyes on the woman again."

Also by Tessa Brookman

Thank you for reading **The Rakish Duke and his Spinster!**

Thank you for being part of this amazing journey!

Also by Tessa Brookman

The Rules of Scandal Series:

The Rakish Duke and his Wallflower

Her Blind Duke

Dukes of Danger Series:

Trapped with the Rakish Duke

The Duke of Scandal

Lost Dukes of London Series:

The Lost Duke and his Staggering Duchess

Seductive Wallflowers Series:

The Duke and the Spoiled Wallflower

A Virgin for the Beastly Duke

About the Author

Born in October 1995, Tessa knows a fair amount about the Regency and Victorian era. Enchanted by the Dukes and Lords, her one fascination has always been writing the stories she wanted to read.

Of course, there's more to life than writing; like taking care of a cat, two dogs, a husband and her endless cravings for adventure and travel. Having traveled to England, Scotland, India and numerous other countries, she has met friends and relatives she never thought she'd meet, with stories too wild to tell.

Her historical romances are here to bring those captivating stories to life with a touch of suspense, intrigue and happily ever afters.

Visit her on the web at www.grovechronicles.com/tessa-brookman

Printed in Great Britain
by Amazon